T0209023

A WALK THROUGH THE VALLEY

Yandell Williams

authorHOUSE®

AuthorHouse™
1663 Liberty Drive
Bloomington, IN 47403
www.authorhouse.com
Phone: 1 (800) 839-8640

Published by AuthorHouse   04/29/2016

ISBN: 978-1-5246-0515-5 (sc)
ISBN: 978-1-5246-0514-8 (e)

Print information available on the last page.

Any people depicted in stock imagery provided by Thinkstock are models, and such images are being used for illustrative purposes only. Certain stock imagery © Thinkstock.

This book is printed on acid-free paper.

Prologue To: A Walk Through The Valley

My beloved said to me, "Rise up my love, my fair one, and come away. For the winter is past, the rain is over and gone. The flowers are springing up and the time of the singing of birds has come. Yes spring is here. The leaves are coming out and the grape vines are in blossom. How delicious they smell! Arise my love, my fair one, and come away."

Song of Solomon, verse 2: 10-13

Love is a state of mind, a feeling, and an experience. When you are in love you feel an inner peace, contentment, you are creative and effective. Life is wonderful. Love brings the happiness that we seek in all of our relationships. By being accepting and appreciative of someone else, we also give them a feeling of well being, of peace, of contentment and warm feelings for us.

The opposite of love is fear and upset. The experience of love for us disappears or dies when someone is critical, non appreciative, and judgmental of us. It is natural for us to shut down, to withdraw into ourselves, to put walls of protection around ourselves. We automatically resist attempts of new love. Eventually, some of us are able to accept the truth of what has happened in our failed relationships, maybe not why, but that it just happened, and we can finally be at peace with the truth. Only then, can we stop resisting. Only then, can we open ourselves up and let ourselves begin to trust again. Until that happens, we cannot move on.

Every great once in awhile a few lucky people find a love that is so strong, so kind, and beautiful that one would wonder if their meeting was pre-destined. Could it be just by chance that two people, with no previous ties or common bond could, out of the clear blue, meet and fall hopelessly and completely in love? Or is it a plan by God, a design for two special people to find a deep and pure love, to find their intended soul mate.

CHAPTER 1

Excitement surged through Avery's veins as she removed the robe that covered her naked body. Goose bumps pricked at the hairs on her arms while she dropped to the cold hardwood floor and crawled under the heavy, gold brocade cloth covering the small oak drum table in the living room of her new home. Peter would be walking up the porch stairs and into the doorway at any moment now.

The new house had a spacious living plan that opened directly from the front door into the living room at the front of the house and the formal dining room with a large oval pecan table placed warmly in front of a massive fireplace at the rear of the room. The kitchen angled off to the left from the dining room just out of sight from the living area. Avery could not hide in the kitchen because she knew Peter would come in there looking for her when she called to him and that would ruin the surprise. The only hiding place she could think of was the covered drum table in the living room just to the right of the front door.

"He better love this!" Avery hoped, and then grinned at how ridiculous she must look crouching naked under a table, hiding from her husband. Her heart pounded like a small child's playing hide and seek at the sound of Peter's footsteps.

Avery met the tall, good looking Peter while they were both attending LSU their freshman year. Peter was a "walk on" for the Tiger's football team. He was a little small for a football scholarship but had won many awards in high school football and the LSU coaches had approached him to come to LSU as a "walk on" hoping that in a year's time he would grow some and buff up even more with all of the equipment the university had available in their sports program. His sandy brown hair and tan skin had made him the heart throb for every girl in high school. And when he smiled, those perfect white teeth made the girls melt. His lean body and massive muscles were only icing on the cake. Peter was not really conceited like a lot of young good looking football stars, he was a little on the shy side but enjoyed the attention, never the less.

Peter was drawn to Avery because she was the new LSU cheerleader that seemed to get all of the attention from the other players, the student body, and the media as well. She was quite stunning with golden blonde hair, streaked with shimmering high lights; large almond shaped brown eyes, flawless golden skin and full sexy lips. She loved life and everyone she met. Peter didn't think he had ever met a friendlier girl. She really wasn't a flirt, like most girls he knew; she just seemed to genuinely like everyone; including him. He didn't quite know what to think when she didn't call or hang around him like most girls did. She didn't have the most voluptuous body he had ever seen, but she was quite attractive with her slim body, round hips, and she had nice sized, upturned breasts for an athletic cheerleader. He would make a point to get to know her better.

The heavy wooden door eased open and the handsome, muscular Peter Lyons stepped into the room and closed the door behind him.

"Peter', Avery called out. "Go take a shower and then come into the kitchen, I have a surprise for you!"

"Where are you, Avery?"

"I'm hiding. I have a great surprise for you, please go upstairs and take a shower and then you can come and get your surprise."

"Damn it, Avery, I don't want to take a shower."

"Please, Peter, you are ruining my surprise!"

Avery could hear Peter shuffling through the mail. When Peter didn't answer Avery said, "Don't worry about the boys, I have a sitter."

"Ok, I'll be downstairs in a few minutes." Peter stated flatly.

Avery listened for Peter's footsteps as he went up the stairs to their bedroom. She eased out from under the drum table and scooted into the kitchen where she had spent the entire afternoon getting this tropical paradise ready for a great surprise for Peter. Avery had pulled two of her large Fichus trees from other parts of the house to place at the head of the large island in her kitchen. She then arranged fresh flowers, fruits and votive candles around the edge of the island. She hurriedly lit the candles and turned backwards to ease herself up onto the island in the space she had left for her naked body.

While she waited for Peter to come into the kitchen she felt a little twinge of fear that he might not like her surprise. Lately he seemed a bit detached. After the birth of their second son, Jason, he seemed different; extremely distant and even critical of everything she and the boys did, or did not do. She assumed that it was due to the extra stress brought on by his added responsibility in his father's business since he was named vice president. At least she hoped that was all it was! Avery never had to worry about her marriage before and she didn't like these thoughts. She had decided to do everything in her power to chase what was wrong with her husband away. And this was the perfect thing to surprise him with and get them back on track!

When Avery heard Peter's footsteps on the staircase, she shook off the uncertainty, leaned back and strategically placed cold grapes over her body as she shivered and giggled in anticipation. What's the matter with me, she thought, what guy wouldn't love a surprise like this!

As Peter walked into the kitchen, Avery threw her head back striking a sexy, sultry, pose. Her long, tanned naked legs stretched to the end of the island; one knee slightly bent. In her deepest, sexiest voice she said "Take me darling."

Peter made a lunge to the kitchen sink, grabbed the pitcher of water in which the flowers had been soaking and threw the water into Avery's face.

Avery sat straight up, grapes falling to the floor, sputtering water as she said to Peter in a hurt and angry tone "What did you do that for?"

"Your hair was on fire, you idiot!" Peter walked out of the room shaking his head and laughing.

CHAPTER 2

Jimmie was standing at the kitchen sink staring at the dirty dishes from the night before. "Why didn't I do these damn things last night?" She mumbled to herself as her mind was whirling about the busy day ahead of her. Jimmie was an executive broker with a small, independent real estate company. Not only had she recently put her own home on the market, she was deep into a couple of deals that she had to get to closing today. Just as she plunged her hands into the dirty water and stuck the first plate into the dishwasher the phone rang. Jimmie grabbed a hand towel lying by the sink and rushed to the phone across the room. The phone usually started ringing around 8:30. This morning it was a little earlier.

"Mom,... it's Avery." "Hey baby, my God, you girls sound more alike every day! What are you up to so early this morning?"

"Everyone tells me I sound like Piper, do I sound like Liza too?"

"Yep, I can hardly tell you girls apart on the phone until we talk a few minutes! And, as you get older, more people tell me how much you look alike, too. One of my tennis buddies told me she saw Piper in Hammond at a tennis tournament and it was you!" Jimmy chirped. Jimmie was very proud of her accomplished and beautiful daughters. Avery was a stock broker at Merrill Lynch and had passed her series 7 test the first time. She had been interning under a senior broker for the past couple of years but was building her own client base now and doing quite well.

"What are you doing today?' Jimmie asked Avery.

"I need to be in the office by 9:00 but I called for your advice, Mom." Jimmie detected a note of concern in Avery's voice.

"What's wrong?" Jimmie asked her daughter.

"Mom, I just don't know what to do about Peter. He has been so hateful to me lately, even short tempered with the boys. Actually, for a really long time, and lately it's just getting worse."

"Well, Avery, do you think he's been under an unusual amount of stress since he took over the company?"

"It could be that to a certain extent, I haven't wanted to tell you but our marriage has been suffering long before he took over the company."

"Like how, Avery?"

"Oh, Mom, I'm walking on eggshells here, being around Peter is like being around a time bomb. I dread when he comes home from work. I make sure I have dinner ready and the house spotless and he still finds something to jump on my case about. I don't have any idea of what the boys or I might say to set him off. He seems so unhappy with us lately.

I've begged him to go to a marriage counselor and his reply is "You knew what I was like before you married me." He refuses to go. I'm at my wits end!

I thought you might be able to give me some of your psychic advice."

"Avery, God knows I've had very similar bouts with your Dad, but usually I can get him to tell me what's bothering him after I badger him for awhile; and talking about it usually puts him in a much better mood. Have you tried to be understanding and let him talk to you about his day?"

"I try and try to get him to talk to me, he acts like I'm and idiot, he just rolls his eyes and totally shuts me out." Mom, I'm getting to the point that I don't think I love him anymore. Here is an example; you know last week when you and Liza and the kids came and spent the night?"

"Yes, did that upset him that we were there?"

"I guess. You know how you and Liza cleaned up the house for me while I went to the school meeting for Hunter and Jason before work? Well, after you guys left to go home, I came in the kitchen and started supper. You had left the house spotless and I was thrilled since the housekeeper wouldn't be here till Friday. Anyway, Peter came in from work and walked into the kitchen and immediately started in on me. He said, "This house is a pig sty! Why didn't you clean it up before you left this morning?"

I said, "Peter, Mother and Liza cleaned this entire house for me before they left! You just show me anything out of place or a speck of dust!"

He looked around and said, "Well, that TV/VCR cord in out of place!"

I said, "Peter, You put that there, and Mother probably thought that's where you wanted it!" Then, he grabbed the newspaper and ignored me the rest of the night. Mother, I have succumbed to begging Peter just to touch me, he just laughs and I end up humiliated and in tears!"

Jimmie could tell that her daughter was crying at the other end of the line.

"Mom, last week he got all of my cell phone records and has accused me of having an affair with my tennis coach!

"Have you been calling Brett?" Jimmie asked.

"Oh, I forgot you met him. Yes, I called him several times last month trying to set our times for the tennis tournament, Peter knew that I've been working on putting this together, but I never dreamed that he could construe something dirty of that! How dare Peter accuse me of such a thing?"

"Avery, I'm so sorry you are going through this, but baby, every marriage has its ups and downs. Try to be patient with him. Try very hard to open the lines of communication, do something exciting and different in the bedroom, maybe which will get him to talk to you. Oh, and for God sakes, stay away from Brett until Peter starts feeling better and more secure about you.

Are you going to be OK?" Jimmie was sick at her stomach and worried about Avery like never before.

"Yes, I'll be ok, and I will try something else. Mother, do you think that I should give up tennis? I've given up so much to make Peter happy, should I give up tennis too because Peter has started this suspicious stuff about me and Brett?"

"Of course you shouldn't! Tennis is great exercise and a wonderful stress relief for you. Just don't give Peter anything to be jealous about!"

"I haven't! I just don't understand why all of a sudden Peter is so jealous." I have never given him a reason to be jealous of me and I never would!" At least Peter has agreed to sit with the boys tonight. I'm going out with Lana and a couple of her friends for dinner and drinks. He seems to like for me to hang out with his sister.

"That will be a nice break for you, and hopefully, things will improve between you and Peter soon!"

"Don't worry, Mom, I'll try more of what you suggested and hopefully, it will all straighten out." Avery knew her mother would worry terribly and hated to call her but felt so much better just talking to someone she knew loved her, someone she knew loved her just the way she was.

Avery Lynch grew up in the small southern town of Lake Providence, Louisiana; she was the middle of three daughters.

The Lynch family was a close, middle class family. The girls were raised in the moral atmosphere of the local Catholic Church. They also attended the catholic school taught by the sisters of Mercy. It was said of Avery that there was never anyone who knew Avery Lynch that didn't love her. She was one of those rare people who had enough self-esteem which allowed her to never take herself too seriously, a great sense of humor, and laughed at her own mistakes. She was also sweet natured and kind with an ability to make everyone around her feel good about themselves. As one friend put it, "Being with Avery just makes me happy!" Avery loved life; she sailed through her childhood and high school years with many friends, she always made good grades and won any competition she went out for. In college, she made cheerleader for the LSU Tigers, was elected their Homecoming Queen, and loved sorority life in the Chi O Mega house on the beautiful LSU campus at Baton Rouge. When Avery met Peter Lyons in college, she thought he was the coolest guy she had ever met.

Peter was good-looking and highly intelligent. Peter came from a very prominent family in Baton Rouge. His father owned a large furniture manufacturing company and had made millions. Peter had one sister and the family lived on a large estate in one of Baton Rouge's newest and nicest subdivisions.

Avery was proud of her small town upbringing in Lake Providence and never felt a twinge of inferiority until she met

Peter. All of her previous boyfriends had put her on a pedestal, like some kind of Goddess which had become very boring and Avery was ready for a challenge in a boyfriend. She found one in Peter Lyons.

She should have been able to see disaster would follow, but she was young and thought Peter was such a good catch. Even when Peter belittled her for being from a "hick" town, and pointed out other girls, telling her she should dress the way they did, she assumed that he was teasing her; after all, Avery knew she had good taste. Those girls Peter wanted her to dress like seemed a little cheap and showed way too much skin!

Avery and Peter seemed to do everything according to the unspoken rules. They dated for three years and Avery was able to keep Peter waiting to have sex, at least until they were engaged. They waited to get married until they both had good jobs after college. And now, after 11 years of marriage, two darling sons in private school, a beautiful home on tree covered acreage in the city, and tons of good friends, thanks to Avery's inviting personality and Peter's money, there seemed to be trouble in paradise.

That evening, Jimmie talked to Bill about her conversation with Avery. Bill sat in his recliner in front of the fireplace with the TV muted. Having raised three daughters, there wasn't much that surprised Bill anymore. He sat silently listening to Jimmie go on about how no matter how thin Avery got, it wasn't thin enough for Peter and no matter that Avery was just featured in a design magazine for decorating the boy's rooms, Peter wouldn't let her have a say in the decor of the rest of the house, he was afraid she would "mess the house up". He had to have a professional decorator.

"You know, Bill, I think the whole problem with Peter is that he is just very self centered. You remember the time when little Hunter was just a baby and there was only enough milk for one bowl of cereal and Peter took it for himself and left the baby with no milk! When Avery told him that they had no more milk for the baby, he continued to pour his milk and admonished Avery for not getting more milk at the store the day before!"

Finally, Bill, who had been deep in thought, and giving no comment about Jimmie's ramblings, suggested Jimmie call Avery in the morning and check on her. It bothered him that Peter did not trust Avery and had checked Avery's phone records, like he was trying to catch her doing something wrong. His comment was so like him, simple country wisdom, and to the point. "You know Jimmie, sometimes, *the smeller is the feller.*

If Peter is checking on Avery's phone records, then he is probably up to no good himself and his guilty conscience is making him check on her to see if she is doing the same thing he is.

The next morning after Jimmie knew that Avery would be home from taking the kids to school, she called. "Hey, Ave, how was your night out last night?" trying to sound upbeat.

"Mom, I'm so glad you called, I have been pacing the floor, what do you make of this? Lana has had a few dates with this new guy and he evidently has a girlfriend that doesn't want to let him go. While we were having dinner this strange girl walked up to Lana and asked if she was, Peter Lyon's sister. Lana told her she was and then the girl said to her,

"Well honey, I'll have you know that your daddy doesn't have enough money for you to buy or steal my boyfriend, so you just stay away from him!" Then she said. *"I don't know why I would expect you to have any more scruples than your brother; he has been cheating on his **wife** for years!"*

"Mother, do you think that's true, do you think that's why Peter has been so distant and hateful to me and the children?" Do you think he could really have a girlfriend?"

"What did Lana say after the girl said that?" Jimmie asked.

"Lana was in shock too, but I think more because the girl verbally attacked her in public than what she said about Peter."

"Avery, I really think that because Peter goes to the bars with the guys a couple of nights a week that there are rumors about Peter. You know how people love to speculate. Has he spent the night out that you didn't know where he was?"

"No, he comes home very late every Tuesday and Thursday but he has never spent the night out unless the guys go to the duck club or something."

"Well, I'm sure that girl has just heard rumors, but I'll tell you this, your dad was concerned that Peter has had your phone records checked. His comment was *sometimes the smeller is the feller.* He thinks you should maybe check his cell phone records. Dad said sometimes a cheater will think that his wife is doing the same thing he is. And if nothing is there, blow it off and try harder to make the marriage work, especially for the children."

"Mom, thanks for calling, I have to run do some things for Junior League this morning. I'll drop by the cell phone company and see if I can get Peter's records today. Daddy has pretty good instincts. At least you and Dad aren't making me feel like I'm crazy."

"OK, baby, keep in touch. Love you."

"Love you too, Mom"

Avery dropped by the cell phone company where she had worked the year before and a couple of years after she and Peter married. She had stayed in touch and still felt that she and the employees of Sundial were pretty good friends, so it wasn't going to be hard to get what she was after. She pulled into the parking lot and sat for a minute wondering if she was doing the right thing.

What if there was nothing on Peter's phone records. She would feel like a total fool. What if there was incriminating evidence on them! Could she handle knowing that Peter was cheating on her? She pretended to be flipping through her day-timer while she decided what she should do.

If Peter is having an affair, I could get aids or something and die, then the children wouldn't have a mother. Shit! I hate him for making me have to suspect him. I Hope to God I won't find anything! Avery composed herself into the happy-go- lucky girl that her ex co-workers identified as Avery. She slid out of the high seat of the Expedition and walked with shoulders erect and head held high into the building through the glass doors of the Sundial office. Fortunately, there were no customers standing at the counter.

"Hey, Scum Bag!" Randall Boggs yelled out at her in his jolly manner.

"Hey Perv!" Avery replied to him.

"Where have you been lately? We've missed you dropping by." Randall was just a year or two older than Avery. He was married to a darling girl and they had three really cute kids, all just a year apart.

"I tried to call you last night but Karen was bathing the kids and she said you were outside doing yard work? You! Yard work, Ha! Avery wrinkled up her nose at Randall like she didn't believe a word of it. "Now I know what scum like you do. You hide in the yard while the woman does all the work!"

Avery loved teasing Randall. He was one of those people with a great sarcastic sense of humor who would never let you get the best of him.

"Yeah, well, you can blame it on Karen; it was a project she invented for me! I loved cleaning out the hot garage, sweating my balls off.! What do you need, Missy?"

"Well, I don't want you to mention this to anyone, but I want to see if I can get a print out of Peter's phone records for the past several months."

"Oh, so you think Peter has let the little man out of the barn, do you?"

"Oh, Randall, I doubt it, I just need to check on some things."

"Yeah, I wouldn't blame you if you **checked on some things**. You probably should have done that a long time ago!"

"Randall, do you know something I don't know?"

"Oh, no, not at all, you know how chickens will cluck, though."

"Randall, you have heard something!" Avery drug Randall back to the corner where no one else could hear them. "Randall, I want to know exactly what you have heard!"

"Easy, darling, I always knew you wanted me but this is too much!" Randall laughed at Avery.

"Really, I haven't heard anything. I tell you what. Let's go get Bobbie to pull his records for you."

"I don't want to get anyone in trouble for this. Do you think Bobbie will mind doing it for me?"

"Oh, I see how you are, you don't mind getting my ass fired, but you want to protect Bobbie." Randall laughed as he led Avery back to Bobbie's office.

"Don't worry about asking Bobbie anything. Her balls are so big, she wouldn't mind asking you to hold them for her if she wanted to do something that took a third hand."

"Wow, that's good to know! Now I remember why I started calling you Perv, you are just nothing but a pervert!" Avery was grinning as they walked into Bobbie's office.

"Hey, Bobbie, pull up Peter Lyon's phone records as far back as the system will let you, would you, please."

"Sure. Hi Avery!" Bobbie seemed glad to see Avery and didn't question at all why they wanted the phone records. Avery watched Bobbie's fingers fly over the keys on her computer's keyboard. Bobbie was a little younger than Avery by a couple of years. She was a little bit of a tomboy, with short brown hair and freckles. Everyone liked her, even though she took no flak off of anyone. Bobbie was all about business. Bobbie handed the sheets that came off of the printer to Avery. "There you go, girlfriend."

"Thank you, Bobbie."

"Sure thing, don't be such a stranger around here!"

"I won't, I promise."

Avery and Randall walked out of the younger girl's office. Randall asked in a more tender voice than Avery knew possible coming from him,

"Do you want me to be with you when you look at these?"

"No, I think I want to go home before I look at them. Randall, you have been such a help, thank you so much."

"Hey, you know I would do anything for you, even if you are a Scum Bag!"

Avery gave a wistful looked back at her friend and smiled as she walked out of the door.

"I really miss you, Randall!" Avery turned away and headed for her Expedition.

Avery sat the papers on the seat next to her and started the car. She kept glancing at the papers dying with curiosity and fear. When she got home, she immediately took the papers into her bedroom and locked the door, even though no one else was there. She sat on the bed and opened the folded papers. It took only a few seconds to see that Peter had been calling one particular number two and three times a day, sometimes even as many as five times a day for the entire three months that she had been able to obtain the phone records. Her heart sank to the deepest pit of her stomach.

Maybe it was a customer he was calling that much. He wouldn't be calling a customer after midnight, would he? The only thing I know to do is to call the number. Avery got up her nerve and dialed the number that showed up so many times on Peter's bill. Avery listened intently as the phone rang once, twice, three times. Then she heard the voice of a young woman.

"You have reached the voice mail of Brandy Smith. Please leave a message, or you can reach me at work at 227-456-8463."

Avery listened to the message again. She then wrote down the number and called it.

"Mercantile Bank and Trust" a voice on the other end of the line answered.

"Oh, uh, hello, I'm sorry, uh, could you please tell me what department Brandy Smith works in?"

"Why, certainly, she is in the insurance department. Hold on while I connect you."

Avery quickly hung up the phone. She felt weak and sick at her stomach.

"*My God, he is cheating on me! I will have to confront him with this. I hate to ruin Father's Day for the children. I'll have to wait till after this weekend. Shit! How am I going to act normal at the lake with Peter's family this entire weekend?* Avery cried herself to sleep and woke up just in time to pick up the boys from school.

During the next few days she found out all she could about Brandy Smith and Peter. It was funny, but after she knew about the affair, it wasn't hard to get people to talk to her about what they knew. They were all sorry that they hadn't told her before, but the story was the same. They just hoped that Peter would come to his senses before she found out about it.

Twenty-year-old Brandy was dating a young intern when she met Peter in a bar. Peter ran around with some of the guys from the bank and they had brought Brandy with them one night while her fiancé was working at the hospital. She was immediately attracted to the brawny, good- looking Peter who had some very good investments in their bank. Of course, Peter loved the attention of the young, adoring girl. His ego was on fire with her attention. Eventually, she must have realized that Peter was not going to leave his wife and children to marry her so she married the unsuspecting intern she was engaged to. It wasn't long, only a couple of months, before she and Peter started seeing each other again.

Avery's heart went out to Brandy's husband, but she was certainly not going to be the one to tell him what his wife was up to.

"That son of a bitch, that stupid girl couldn't she get the hint the first time? Sure, Peter was seeing her now; she wasn't a threat to his marriage if she was married too! What an ASS!"

After a miserable weekend at the family's lake house, Avery felt it was time to let Peter know that she knew all about the two-year affair. Avery held onto a shred of hope that it was all a miserable mistake, but when she told Peter that someone told her he was having an affair, he said,

"Who told you that, did Brandy?" Avery had not mentioned a name and knew it was true by the mention of her name. It was a horrible scene with Peter and Avery yelling at each other. Avery's tears and anger only seemed to make Peter defiant. He admitted to the affair but blamed Avery for not giving him what he needed.

"What in the hell could you have possibly needed from me that I wasn't giving to you, Peter?" Avery screamed at him.

"Was it sex? Huh, Peter, was it sex?" Peter ignored her. "It couldn't have been sex, I never denied you sex, in fact, I tried to think of fun things to do in the bedroom, Peter!"

"You just weren't giving me what I needed, Avery! You worked on that stupid Christmas bizarre thing, for one thing and left me at home with the boys every night last Christmas, Avery!"

"Peter that was a whole year after you started the affair! What a stupid excuse!"

"That was an example, Avery."

"Well, it was a terrible example, Peter."

"I'm just saying that there had to be something you were not giving me at home or I wouldn't have wanted to find someone else."

"Get out, Peter, I want you out of here!" Screeched Avery.

Peter began ignoring Avery, like she had not even been fighting with him. She had no choice but to sleep on the couch and ignore him back.

The next morning when Avery returned home from taking the kids to school, Peter was still at home lingering over his coffee and reading the paper after he had eaten his bowl of cereal, just as though nothing had happened between the two of them last night. It seemed like a bad dream to Avery. Peter actually thought that she would just get over it if he ignored her. She called an attorney in front of him to make an appointment. Peter said nothing but left for work during her conversation with the attorney.

During the next few days, after Peter realized that Avery was serious, he started trying to talk her into staying in the marriage.

"Come on Ave, please get over this and let's work things out. It really didn't mean anything to me. Come on, I'm sorry! I didn't do anything you didn't do."

"Peter, do you realize that you can't even say that you are sorry without trying to blame me!"

"I just know that I haven't done anything any worse than what everyone else has done, and I know that you had an emotional affair, even if it wasn't physical with Bret!"

"That excuse is just not good enough, Peter, and it is also very untrue! I want a divorce! I want you out of here!"

Peter refused to leave, but that evening Peter moved his things into the other bedroom. After the move was completed, Peter and Avery sat down on the couch, each with a child in their lap. Peter started by asking the boys if they were wondering why he was moving his clothes into another room. Of course, Hunter had already been asking. Peter said it would probably only be for a little while.

"But why, Daddy, don't you like Mommy anymore?"

Peter started crying. Avery's quick response was tinted with sorrow and anger for Peter,

"Of course your Daddy and I still like each other very much. It's just that we have been arguing a lot lately. You know, fussing at each other. We think that we will get along better if we stay apart for awhile." Tears began streaming down Hunter's little face and seeing Hunter cry Jason started to cry too. Avery, Peter, Hunter and Jason held each other and cried together until the little boys fell asleep in their parent's laps.

"See, Avery, this will destroy the children!" Peter said accusingly at Avery. "We need to go to counseling and work this out!"

"I wish you would have thought of this before you took up with another woman, what did you think you were doing? Did you never consider how this would hurt the kids, not to mention me?"

"I never did anything you didn't do!" barked Peter.

"My God, Peter, I never went out and found a boyfriend, and please quit trying to say I did just to make you feel better!"

Avery went to her room and cried herself to sleep too. The next morning she agreed to go to marriage counseling with him as long as he stayed away from her.

Twice a week, for two months, they met at the counselor's office. Their first sessions were angry, bitter, accusations. It seemed that each session the same old arguments arose that were going nowhere. Peter said that Avery didn't give him what he needed, but he couldn't pinpoint what he did need. Avery argued that she had begged him to go to a marriage counselor years ago when she felt him becoming distant, but he wouldn't. He said the past didn't matter, that he was willing to work on the marriage now. He continued to use that same old adage that he hadn't done anything any worse than anyone else had done.

Avery agonized over what to do. She felt so terribly torn, betrayed, guilty and so terribly sad for the children. She also felt humiliated, embarrassed, and angry with Peter for his infidelity and for not trying to fix the marriage before he brought in another woman. She could not understand why he didn't seem remorseful, why he thought everyone else seemed to be unfaithful to their wives. Never the less, she had just about decided to stay and try to make the marriage work when she got a phone call one morning just as she walked in the door from taking the kids to school.

"Is this Mrs. Peter Lyons?"

"Yes, it is."

"Avery, uh, Mrs. Lyons, I hate to call you, but I am Tim Smith, Brandy's husband. Do you know who Brandy is?" Avery's heart sank when the voice on the other end of the phone became one of shocked recognition, someone with whom Avery had so much in common. It was as if she were talking to a brother, someone she cared for. "Yes, Tim, I know who Brandy is."

"She told me she was in love with your husband and they were going to get married. Do you know about this?"

"Well, Tim, that is not the story I have been hearing, I have heard all about the affair, but Peter has been begging me to come back into the marriage. He obviously has been telling Brandy something different."

"Avery, uh, Mrs. Lyons, I feel so bad for calling. I just had to hear it from someone else, I guess. She told me she is sick of living with me while I am in residency and she is tired of working. She told me she wants to go to the club and play golf everyday, she wants to belong to Junior League and all of the things you do. I told her if she could just wait a little while longer, she could have anything she wants. My God, Mrs. Lyons, do you know how much earning potential I have as a plastic surgeon?"

"Tim, you can call me Avery, and I am so sorry. I know you haven't been married very long. Did you know that she was seeing Peter before you were married?"

"I knew nothing until last night when she confessed everything and asked for a divorce. We started dating in high school, I adored her, I thought she loved me."

Avery's heart ached for Tim,

"Tim, I am so very sorry. I am sorry for you and I am sorry for myself, and most of all, I am sorry for my sons. I have been looking for a sign whether to go or stay, you will never know how much I appreciate your call. You know what? You deserve so much better than a woman who only thinks of herself and material things. I know it hurts now, but I believe you and I will both be better off without Peter and Brandy in our lives."

At the next counseling session, Avery asked Peter in front of the counselor if he had given up his girlfriend. He answered honestly, this time, and said,

"No, but the only reason I am still seeing her is that if you don't come back into the marriage, I will be left with no one. But, I promise, Avery, she doesn't mean anything to me."

At that statement Avery stood up and calmly said to Peter,

"You are telling me that you don't care at all about someone you have been seeing for two and a half years, someone you called at least seventy times a month on the phone; her voice began to rise to a higher, angrier pitch. "Someone you spent several hours on the phone with at my parent's home last Christmas? Someone who just asked her husband for a divorce so she could marry you! Well, Peter Lyons, you have just made me realize something very important! You haven't hurt me;

you have done me a great favor! You are one cold, lying son of a bitch! I feel sorry for Brandy!"

Avery turned, walked out of the counselor's office, drove straight to her attorney's office and filed for divorce.

The divorce process seemed long and ugly, but took only three months to become final. She thought she would be sad the day her divorce was final, but that November day, just after Thanksgiving, was a freeing experience for Avery. She no longer felt tied to a controlling man. She was a new woman and anxious to start her new life as a single mother to her sons. Time started to fly by for Avery and the boys.

Avery sold her share of the house to Peter and she and the boys moved to an apartment while Avery and her shopped for and bought a cute little house near the same neighborhood as their old house. The new house was a gray, two-story saltbox style with a large covered front porch and red brick steps leading up to a cheery, red front door. The interior was much smaller than the house they had shared with Peter, but adequate for Avery and her sons.

She loved the kitchen best of all. It had wood plank flooring and windows that wrapped around two sides of the room. The master suite was down stairs next to the kitchen. It was a much smaller than she had been used to but would suffice. The bath would not. It would have to be totally torn out and remodeled. Three other bedrooms were upstairs, which was perfect for when her mother and sisters came for a weekend.

Avery's immediate goal was to make life for her sons as regular and normal as possible. Right now that meant to make as many trips from the apartment to the house with as much as she and little boys could carry until all of their personal belongings were moved.

Every night after the trips to the apartment, she would put the boys to bed on a soft pallet on the floor in their empty new bedrooms. After prayers and a story or two, she would stay up into the wee hours of the morning painting and cleaning in order to have the house ready for the movers to bring their furniture the week before Christmas. After the furniture was in place, they would hop in the car and head to Lake Providence for a week of rest and relaxation over the Christmas holidays. She didn't have to have the boys back to Peter until Christmas day.

Every once in awhile, in a tired or lonely moment, Avery would feel a familiar stab of pain and sorrow in her heart that soon would turn to anger at Peter for destroying the family life that she had put so much of herself into for Peter and the boys. Those moments were surfacing less often and most of the time she was happy to be out of the marriage. Peter had been so controlling that she felt a freedom that she hadn't felt in years.

It was one of these evenings after the boys were tucked in and Avery was painting the upstairs bathroom when the phone rang.

"Hello" Avery was frustrated having to stop to answer the phone. She assumed it was Peter calling again to make arrangements to get the boys this weekend.

"Avery, hey, this is Julie, I have a favor to ask you."

"Sure, what is it?" Avery asked. Avery loved Julie Kramer; they met through their boys at school. Julie had two sons the same ages as eight year old Hunter and five year old Jason.

"Jim and I are having a Christmas dinner party next Thursday night for the doctors and nurses at the office and I..."

"No problem, Julie, I will be happy to let the boys spend the night over here and I'll take them to school Friday morning, you and Jim can sleep late!"

"No, Avery, I have a sitter for the boys, I want to fix you up with Jim's partner in the clinic. He needs a date."

"Oh, Julie, I really don't want to meet anyone right now. I have so much going on in my life and I am perfectly happy with just the little guys and me. Thank you for thinking of me though." Avery, this guy is really the sweetest guy! I have known him for years and he is really so nice. He has two sons and has been divorced for a couple of years. He is not dating anyone and I've told him all about you. Please, please, please, do it for me. I'll never try to fix you up again if you just do this for me this time, I promise."

"Whoa girl, you sure know how to put the squeeze on someone. I tell you what, I'll try to find a sitter and I'll let you know tomorrow, OK?"

"Great! His name is Grant Jones. He is so cute and sweet. He really got a raw deal from his ex-wife too. I know you will have a good time. Got to run, I'd love to help you paint, but I've got a million things to do to get ready for this party!"

"Gee, thanks, Julie. I'll call you tomorrow."

Avery hung up and stood staring at the phone. A feeling of dread washed over her that she couldn't shake.

I really don't want to go out with anyone right now, she thought, *especially a cocky cardiologist! I doubt that he is cute, either!*

It wasn't that Avery didn't ever want another man in her life, she thought she might one day be ready to meet someone, but certainly not yet! She had leaned on Brett during the separation and pending divorce because he was there, he was the one who filled her need to be told how beautiful and desirable she was, but she broke the ties with him when she realized he

Was wanting more from the relationship than she was ready for. She had guilt feelings about using him, she hated hurting him, but she knew that a relationship based on need would never work. It was ironic that the very person Peter accused her of having an affair with, when absolutely nothing of the sort crossed her mind, was the very person she leaned on when she found out about Peter's betrayal.

Avery had made her mind up, she didn't need a man, she was perfectly happy by herself with the boys. They could do anything they wanted to, they could watch what they wanted to on TV, they could all cuddle up in her bed and eat crackers and popcorn, and, if she wanted to paint the kitchen purple in her new house, she could!

Nope, I do not want another man in my life right now; besides, I don't have time to fool with this party! Ha! What am I worrying about, it's just a favor for Julie, I'll go to the party, be nice to Jim's partner, then that will be that, if I can find a sitter!

Avery really liked Julie. She was tiny with honey blonde hair and the most innocent eyes. Her blue eyes danced when she smiled with mischief but Avery often thought Julie was very reserved for such a beautiful girl. Avery teased Julie often about how she must have gotten away with murder when she was a child with that innocent face. Avery smiled when she thought how different she and Julie were. They met through their boys at school and Avery found out that Julie had married a boy from Avery's home town. Her parents even knew Jim's parents. He was now a cardiologist in Baton Rouge. Both girls were transplants to Baton Rough and even though they were so different, they seemed to have more in common than with other new friends Avery had met.

They were both mothers of two rambunctious boys and they took the boys at least weekly to play in the park after school. Julie was totally repulsed by torn, dirty jeans and wriggly worms falling out of those jeans pockets and horrified when Avery pulled the worms from their pockets and pretended to eat them. After the horror show, Julie would instruct her sons to please be very careful with the worms, but to remove them and put them back in the loose dirt very gently so as not to hurt them.

Avery did try to find a sitter, she at least called her favorite sitter, but she was busy next Thursday night so Avery called Julie to tell her the bad news.

"Hey, Julie, it's Avery, I couldn't find a sitter for Thursday night. I'm really sorry, but I must say I'm a little relieved too, ha! Thursday is the day the movers are bringing my furniture and I will be swamped!" Maybe you could call Lana to go out with this Grant guy. She is the resident date queen lately"

"Oh, no you don't, Avery, I have already told him that *you* were going to be his date. I am going to pick your kids up after school and have *my* sitter take them to McDonalds then; they can play here with my boys until after the party. You just have to do this for me, Avery!"

Avery sat silent on the line for a few minuets,

"Avery, *please....*"

"Oh, all right, Julie, but why is it so important to you that *I* be the one to come with him?"

"Avery, I just know that you two will hit it off. You really have a lot in common. You are really very much alike in a lot of ways."

"If you say so, are you going to have him call me or what?"

"Yes, I'm sure he will call you.....I love you for this!"

"You owe me, Julie Kramer!"

Avery worked hard the rest of the weekend and all the next week getting the house ready for the furniture. She had carpenters coming the week after Christmas to expand the small bathroom in the master suite, so she let the little boys help her knock out the walls of the existing closet. Each day after school, Hunter and Jason would hurry to get their homework done, then,

Avery and the boys would race to get their favorite hammer and tear into the bathroom where they would bang, hammer and chip away at the tile in the shower and walls that had to come down. It was sheer heaven for the boys. They had never been allowed to tear up anything in the house, and now, they were actually getting to knock out walls! Little Jason would bang the wall about waist level with his child sized hammer, then duck. Hunter and Avery would bend over laughing at his antics. It was the most fun the boys could ever remember having inside. The little boys felt big and strong and relished the thought that their mother trusted them to be able to do something grown- ups usually did. They loved getting to be part of the remodeling team and they adored their mother.

Moving day turned out to be a beautiful sunny day. The morning air was crisp, but not too cold. The movers were sitting in Avery's driveway when she returned from taking the kids to school. She rushed to unlock the doors for them and found her best friend Janie waiting on the back deck for her, sprawled in a lawn chair with one petite, jeans clad leg over the arm and two cups of steaming coffee in each hand. She had wrapped herself in a garage sale bedspread from the nearest box in the carport for warmth,

"Janie, you angel!, Avery squealed in delight.

"Hey, what are friends for; let's get this show on the road!"

The girls contemplated the placement of the furniture while the movers tried to be patient and do just what the ladies wanted. Janie had a flair for furniture placement and Avery was happy to have Janie's suggestions since she was uncertain of her on abilities lately.

Around noon, Avery dashed out to pick up lunch for everyone and was grateful that Julie was picking up Jason from kindergarten and Hunter at 3:00. She would be able to work all day without having to leave again.

When she returned with lunch, her friend, and real estate agent, Lisa was there with Janie having the movers change the placement of the desk for the third time!

At six o'clock that evening, Avery looked up from a large box of paintings and pictures she was unpacking. Fear seemed to seize her as she froze in place as the memory entered her mind. She screamed to the other two girls,

"Oh, my God, I have to be ready in thirty minutes; I have a date! How in the world am I going to do this! I have nothing to wear! All of my clothes are packed!"

"Why didn't you tell me you had a date?" cried Janie with a hurt pout on her pretty lips.

"I really forgot about it. Or, maybe I tried to forget about it. That is why Julie has the kids, so I would come to her office party with this guy!" Avery laughed at her friend for pouting.

"And I thought she was just being considerate of you during your move!" Julie rolled her eyes.

"Who is the date with?" Asked Lisa

"Oh, it's some partner of Jim Kramer. I believe his name is Grant Jones, at least I hope that is his name!"

"Grant Jones!" Lisa screamed. "My God, Avery, do you realize what a great catch he would be?"

"Do you know him, Lisa?" Avery was surprised that Lisa might know him.

"No, not really, I have just heard great things about him. What a catch, girl!"

"I don't want to catch anyone. I just promised Julie I would go tonight for her and he will be here any minute now, what am I going to do?"

"I'll tell you what you are going to do, run jump in the shower and I'll run to my house and grab an outfit and some makeup. I need to pick my girls up anyway and Lisa can stay here to finish up with the movers." Janie's take-charge personality was galloping to the occasion.

"Lisa, is that all right with you?" Avery asked her friend.

"Of course, it's all right with me, now go hop in the shower, for

God's sake!"

By the time Avery got out of the shower, Janie was back with the wardrobe.

"Here, let me blow-dry your hair while you slip on your underwear." ordered Janie.

"I can't believe I agreed to go tonight!" complained Avery as she and Janie worked in unison trying to put makeup on, hair in rollers and pull up a pair of new panty hose over Avery's damp behind.

"Avery, you are going to look like a million dollars, relax, we have five more minutes."

Just at that moment, Lisa came breathless into the upstairs room where the girls were dressing.

"Oh, my God, Avery, he's here and he is *DARLING!*

Avery and Janie quickly finished their makeover and a few minutes later Avery was headed for the stairs to meet her date for the night. She turned to look back at her friends who were coaxing her on and gave them a grimace that showed them how nervous she really was. She stopped to say

"I love you guys, what would I have done without you!"

The girls scowled and motioned to her to go on and quit stalling.

Avery took a deep breath and started the decent down the stairway. She found herself holding tightly onto the stair railing to steady herself. When she reached the bottom of the stairs, she took a deep breath and turned to smile at the stranger sitting on her couch in the living room.

"Hi, she said, you must be Grant."

Grant stood up when he heard his name and turned to see one of the most beautiful women he had ever seen. He stood with his mouth open to speak but no words seemed to come. Finally,

"And you must be Avery."

He was pleased to notice that her reaction to him seemed to be as pleasant a surprise as well.

Avery was shocked that Grant was so handsome; Julie had said he was cute, but other people she had met that knew Grant Jones had told her how nice he was, but didn't give the impression that they thought he was handsome. One acquaintance she had bumped into in a dress shop said

"I heard you are coming to the office party with Dr. Jones."

"Yes, I promised Julie I would come. I hope he is gorgeous?" Avery teased her friend in a questioning way.

"Well, he is not gorgeous, but he is tall and very nice!" *That's scary, thought Avery!*

Now, that the meeting was here, she was not at all prepared for what she was seeing! He was tall, over 6 feet, and slim, with dark brown hair and rounded brown eyes emanating a kindness and warmth that Avery had not expected, but the thing that captured Avery's attention the most was his well defined full lips, nice teeth and easy smile. She was shocked and a little ashamed of herself, she thought he was beautiful.

"I brought a bottle of wine, I hope you like a cabernet."

"Oh, how nice, I'll get some wine glasses, if I can find any; the movers just brought my furniture today. Would you mind plastic cups?" *How embarrassing!* Avery thought as she dug in a bottom drawer of the kitchen for a couple of plastic Scooby Doo cups. Avery returned to the living room with the plastic cups looking a little sheepish.

"Hey, this is great, Grant said enthusiastically. "I have two sons who love Scooby too!"

With that, the tension vanished and they both laughed as Grant poured the wine into the cups.

Janie and Lisa had been eavesdropping and snickering at the top of the stairs. They decided that things were going well, and it was time for them to leave. They descended to the living room to meet Grant and to say their good buys. Avery introduced them and Grant offered them a cup of wine.

"Thanks, but no thanks" said Lisa.

Janie spoke up "It was nice to meet you, Grant, we've got to run."

Avery walked her friends to the front door and thanked them both again for *all* of their help.

"I'll call you first thing in the morning." Janie called over her shoulder as she winked at Avery. Then to Grant, "take care of our girl." as the door closed behind them.

Blushing slightly, Avery walked back over to Grant with her wine cup in her hand.

"Would you like a tour of my new house while we drink our wine."

"Sure, I'm impressed already!"

The Christmas party at Jim and Julie's home was a wonderful change from Avery's routine. She felt at ease with Grant. He had a most charming personality and was very considerate of her the whole evening, introducing her to the office staff and making sure that she didn't need a thing. He stayed close to her without hovering and, occasionally would put his hand on her back leading her to another group of people to talk to. She caught him looking at her several times and once after dinner, she found him starring at her. She began thinking that she could easily get used to this! The attention was making her blush,

"What?" she said smiling.

"What are you looking at, do I have something on my face?" she asked laughing.

"No, no, I was just wondering what in the hell was Peter Lyons thinking when he let you go!"

"Oh, you just don't know me; I'm very mean and a little crazy too!" Avery teased.

"Well, you are a very ***beautiful*** mean and crazy girl, if you don't mind me saying."

"Thank you, that is very sweet of you to say." *Was this man for real?*

CHAPTER 3

Grant Lee Jones had put himself through college on student loans and had attended Tulane Medical School in New Orleans after graduating from Georgia Tech. There he met an attractive student nurse named Tara, the only child of wealthy family from New Orleans. He should have been able to see the signs that a long- term relationship might not work with Tara. She was very demanding and they fought often during their courtship, but he was ready to settle down, he wanted a home and family, so they married during the 1st year of his residency.

Grant didn't mind a bit that his wife's financial future was of great magnitude. Tara's father was one of the wealthiest men in New Orleans and even though he would never admit to it, her fathers great wealth made her more appealing.

Soon after the marriage, however, he began to realize that maybe he had made a mistake. His wife became increasingly demanding, she did not try to hide the fact that she was very spoiled and self-centered.

Grant tried hard to please her; gave in to her whims and catered to her while trying to keep his sanity during his internship, but nothing he did seemed to please her. If

41

the smallest thing didn't go her way she would fly into a screaming rage.

She learned what buttons to push and how to control him. Not long into the marriage, Grant regretted that he had not waited until he really got to know Tara before making a lifelong commitment.

By the time he came to this realization it was too late. She was pregnant. Because Grant came from a broken home, he vowed that he would never put his own children through the pain he had suffered because of divorce.

Tara played on his soft heart and good nature and he let her control him to keep the peace. His diagnosis of her behavior was that she was narcissistic and his medical background helped him to excuse her behavior as something she could not control.

Their first born was a beautiful baby boy with jet-black hair, smooth, dark skin and big dark eyes. His coloring was like his mother's who was 5th generation New Orleans. That meant that she was of Italian and French decent with dark skin, hair and eyes. Her family's wealth prevented her from being called a "Cajin".

They named their first- born Travis and both delighted in their baby's antics. Three years later, Trent was born. He looked much more like his father, especially in his coloring. He was a long and thinner baby than Travis with lighter skin, brown hair and big, round, brown eyes. Both boys inherited their father's pretty mouth and his calm disposition.

The boys became the most important thing in Grant's life. He doted on his children and let them fill the void of his unhappy marriage.

As the boys got older, Tara's disposition just got worse. She constantly complained about Grant to her friends that he was boring, that he spent too much time at work or that he spoiled the boys by playing with them too much. She resented the time he spent with them.

Tara belittled Grant and nagged him about every little thing. Once, when Grant took Tara on a business trip to New York, he accidentally left a magazine in the seat of a taxi taking them to the airport. Tara decided to read an article and when she discovered Grant had lost the magazine, she ranted the entire ride home about how irresponsible and thoughtless Grant was for doing such a thing to her! She was certain he did it on purpose!

"Grant, you left that book on the seat just so that I couldn't have anything to read on the plane." You are mean and hateful!"

Grant felt like an unappreciated servant most of the time. Eventually he withdrew. Still, occasionally, he made attempts to include her in his life. He invited her to go to medical conferences and to take trips with him and the boys, but she very seldom wanted to go.

Grant often thought how wonderful it would be to have more children, but Tara was quick to take her frustrations out on the children as well as Grant. He could handle the harassment she made him endure, but he couldn't stand her verbal abuse of the boys so another child was out of the question.

After the boys started school, the couple grew further and further apart.

In order to cope, Grant became consumed with his work at the clinic and on his days off or vacation times he would take the boys somewhere that he knew would be fun for them. Although Tara had millions at her disposal in her trust account, she kept nursing to get away from the children and she spent the rest of her time playing golf with her friends at the club.

To all on the outside, she was a devoted mother seemingly wanting the best for her children, which usually was a positive reflection on her.

Grant knew that she loved the boys, but she was bossy and controlling and Grant or the boys couldn't take being around her too much without some private time.

Grant wished she could be more relaxed and fun with the boys but any mention of this to Tara would set her off on another tantrum about how **someone** had to be the adult and teach them responsibility, that he sure as hell wasn't capable of doing it!

Dr. Grant Jones breezed through his residency; all of his patients seemed to love him and they referred more patients to him than he could see. He could not understand why he could get no respect from his own wife!

Grant felt that the failure of their marriage, in some way, must be his fault. Grants father had left home while he and his brother and sister were young.

After he left, Grant saw his father seldom. To him, his father deserted them and a failed marriage must be the man's fault. He convinced Tara to go to a marriage councilor for the sake of the children; she saw no need but agreed to go just to shut him up and for nearly two years they attended weekly sessions. It was during this time that Grant came home to rest after a tough surgery, only to find his wife in bed with another man!

This was the final straw. It was pretty degrading to Grant to have the wife of a hard-working heart surgeon banging the tennis pro from his own country club, and he was paying him to do it! It finally dawned on him that he had done all he could possibly do to make their marriage work, and maybe, just maybe it really wasn't all his fault that it wasn't working. He filed for divorce and started his new life as a single man.

Grant found himself much more at peace. At times he was lonely, but that was usually when the boys were with their mother and he was not on call. He did enjoy reading and if the house felt too empty, he would head down to the local

Books a Million and sip coffee at Joe Muggs while he enjoyed a good article or book or he would go running.

Grant could not believe that this blind date had turned out to be so great!

He had dated some in the two years sense his divorce, but women who made appointments for EKGs just to meet him were totally out of the question. He would not date any of his patients. The one girl, Suzanne, that he had dated for any length of time was an off and on again thing. She was a sweet and pretty girl and very smart. She was a journalist for the local paper, but there was just no real spark. Maybe that is why he never got around to introducing her to his sons.

Grant was becoming increasingly needy and lonely, and she filled the need, but when she started pushing for marriage and children, Grant had to break off the relationship. He knew he was not in love and he was not about to make the same mistake twice!.

Grant became more and more successful and built quiet a reputation for himself as one of the top cardiologists in Louisiana. He was appointed to various positions in the state cardiologist's association, and he was on the board of trustees at the Baton Rouge hospital.

His private practice kept him busy, but every other weekend and every Wednesday night he got to have the boys. That was the highlight of his life. Grant made the best of being a bachelor, but something was missing. He was lonely.

He missed his boys; he couldn't understand why he couldn't find someone he could care for and someone who would love and appreciate him. He loved the idea of having a home and family. He longed for a normal family again.

To avoid going home to an empty house, he stopped by the Books-A-Million after work more often than not, browsing through the isles of music CDs or trying to find a good book to read. He did enjoy having a coffee and watching the people, and it sure beat the hell out of the alternative.

Grant dated off and on. Usually someone would "fix him up" but nothing ever seemed to work out. He was starting to hate blind dates; he wondered what in the hell made him feel so compelled to go on this one.

The fact that Julie Kramer had told him so many nice things about Avery made him *kind of* excited about it, but all women said wonderful things about a girl they wanted to pair him with. He was sure Julie was no different, but his expectations were usually as high as the "would be Cupid's" description of the blind date, then, only to be disappointed when he met her. This time he was not going to expect anything except to be glad he didn't have to go to this year's office party alone.

What a shock! This girl, Avery, was a natural beauty with honey colored hair, highlighted streaks, in a smooth, classic, shoulder length style. High cheekbones, dark, almond shaped eyes and a beautiful smile with full lips and white teeth. Her skin had a golden glow, soft and flawless, the type of skin that would tan easily; yet, she was not really dark like most of the Italian girls he had met in Louisiana. She looked more like the girls back home in Georga. She was slim, but with a curvy figure that would make any man stare.

She was a little feisty and fun yet gracious and friendly and handled herself with a poise that impressed him, especially around people at the party that she didn't know. He couldn't quit looking at her.

I wonder why in the world her husband would cheat on her, is something wrong with her that I don't see, he thought. Just then, Avery interrupted his thoughts. "What?, what are you starring at? Is something on my face?"

"No, no, I was just wondering what in hell was Peter Lyons thinking when he let you go!" He couldn't believe he had just said that!

Avery laughed and said, "Well, I've heard that I am really mean and crazy too, so don't let yourself be fooled. That is a very sweet thing for you to say though, thank you." Avery looked down at her wine glass, running her fingers around the rim of the glass as she said shyly, "I was just wondering how anyone could have hurt someone as kind as you."

"Thank you, Avery, that's a sweet thing for you to say. I guess Julie has filled us both in on our illustrious pasts" Grant was touched; he couldn't remember anyone thinking of his feelings like that besides his mother or Gram. He could tell that Avery was sincere, and to him, her sincerity in that statement lifted his spirits through the roof.

The evening progressed beautifully. Grant loved the light flirting Avery aimed at him and he loved the way she stayed near him without hanging.

Avery admired his calm demeanor and easy smile. They found each other easy to talk to. Avery seemed very alive at this party. She had no problems carrying on conversations with complete strangers. Grant enjoyed the party but was a little more reserved than Avery. He enjoyed watching her talk to the other party guests. Her animated personality was charming; the fact was he just enjoyed watching **her.**

Neither of them were ready to end the evening, but as one of the last couples at the party, the inevitable ending had to come.

Avery had been exhausted from her long day of moving, but strangely, the party had revived her. As people were saying their good byes, Grant leaned over to her and said, "I'm anxious to meet your boys."

Julie and Jim had given all of the children strict orders to stay in the playroom with the sitter during the party. They had been so occupied playing that they never even tried to come downstairs.

Avery looked at her watch, "I really need to get them home and in bed, they have school tomorrow. Come help me tear them away from Julie's kids. I'll introduce you then...

I hope you don't mind taking us all home." Avery felt a little uncomfortable having Grant take them home, she hated imposing and she knew he must be tired, she was wishing she had brought her own car and met him at the party.

The drive home turned out to be very pleasant. Grant seemed to know how to put Avery at ease. Grant and Avery talked and laughed about some of the people at the party. Jason and Hunter slept peacefully in the back seat of the car. They fell asleep the minute the car engine started.

Once in the driveway of her home, Avery hopped out of the car and opened the back door to wake the boys. Grant surprised her by coming around the car to stand beside her, he said, "Don't wake them, if you can carry the little one, I can carry the big one. What's his name again?"

"Hunter." Avery whispered and they carried the sleeping boys up the stairs together and gently laid them in their beds.

They tiptoed down stairs and Avery asked Grant if he would like another glass of wine.

"No, thanks, I've got an early surgery, but I would like to call you sometime, if that's all right."

Avery could feel her heart quicken slightly. "I would like that. And, by the way, thank you for a wonderful evening, and for the wine. I had a great time." Avery said as she looked up at him smiling while walking him to the kitchen door.

Grant surprised her by turning around to face her instead of walking out of the door. Without a word, and before she realized what was happening, he leaned into her and put his hands high on her back. They spread a warmth through her body as they covered her entire back. His eyes were smiling and he seemed confident as he pulled her to him. Avery had no time to react. His arms were strong, but gentle as he pulled her close and leaned in to kiss her. Avery parted her lips and felt herself weaken as their lips met. His full lips were soft and warm; his embrace was all ncompassing and made Avery feel safe and warm. His kiss became more passionate and Avery felt herself reeling as if about to faint. He felt a rush of passion he had not allowed himself to feel in quite a long time. Grant then pulled back and kissed her once more on the cheek. "I had a great time too." He said, and then he turned and walked out the door.

Avery stood for a moment in a daze. When she gained some composer, she felt her hands shake as she tried several times to twist the lock of the back door. She turned around and let her back fall against the door, her heart beating wildly. *My God, what has just happened to me? I must be really starved for attention!*

Avery had a hard time getting to sleep that night. Thoughts of Grant Jones kept running through her head. *Not long ago Mom asked me exactly what I wanted in a man, let me see....I wanted someone kind, very kind, someone who loved children, someone considerate of others, not just of me, someone who wouldn't run when he found out that I have children, someone who could be a real friend to me, as well as a lover. Someone with some of the same interests as I, and someone who wouldn't be too serious, someone who I could really have fun with, and someone who would really let me love him. Mom laughed and told me that Walt Disney had died. She was probably right. Grant was a wonderful date, but that was all it was. What am I thinking, one little kiss and I go nuts! I am not wanting a man in my life right now, even if Grant Jones does seem to have all of those qualities!*

My God, he's a doctor. I'm sure he is a huge ladies man and probably cocky as hell, although he didn't seem cocky. That's right, Avery, you've never met a doctor worth dating! He must have been on his best behavior!

Her last thoughts as she drifted off to sleep were, *Oh well, it was a wonderful date, he was a great kisser, and he certainly was very attentive, he made me feel like Cinda-freeking-rella!* Avery chuckled at herself for thinking of her favorite line from "Pretty Woman to describe her own date." a little nicer language, though.

Avery awoke to her alarm at 7:00 a.m. "Time to get up kids. Yahoo! It's the last day of school and tomorrow, after your basketball game, Hunter, we are going to MeMe and PaPa's for Christmas! Jason, come on, hop in the shower and I'll start breakfast, OK guys?" Avery knew the boys were tired. She knew she would have to keep after them to get them ready for school on time.

After dropping the boys off, Avery decided to do a little shopping. The December day was cool, but not cold enough to wear a coat, the sun was shining and Avery found herself in the Christmas Spirit for the first time this whole season. Her shopping took some serious thought and her time was limited. She would have to go back to school and get Jason at noon. She hardly thought of Grant Jones the whole morning, well, not every moment at least!

As Avery and Jason were pulling into the driveway around noon, something caught little Jason's eyes. "Mom! Thewe is a Pwesant on the font powch!"

"Jason, remind Mommie to call that teacher for your speech today. She is so cool, you are going to LOVE her, and we will have her start teaching you when school starts again." Avery thought Jason's speech impediment was adorable, but she didn't want him going into first grade not able to say his Rs. "But Mommie, thewe willy is a pweasant!"

"OK, Sweety, we'll go see what it is."

Jason jumped from the car and ran to the front porch with Avery on his heels. "It's a Chwistmas thing, Mom!

Avery opened the card attached to the beautiful Christmas Wreath adorned with sugared fruit leaning against her front door. The card read:

Thank you again for a lovely evening. Will you have dinner with me when you get back from your parent's home, say, the day after Christmas? I'll call you soon.

Signed: Grant Jones.

"Mom!"

"Hey, Avery! are you all packed and ready to come home?"

"Yes, but we have to run by and take care of something first, so we will be just a little late getting there. Just don't want you to worry."

"That's fine, just drive carefully. Hey, how was your date last night?"

"Oh, my God, Mom, I'm in **love**, I am going to marry him!"

"Ha! Does he know that yet?"

"Of course not, but I'm sure it's love! Ha!"

"Yea, Yea, I remember this same kind of conversation when you were dating in college. Ha! Every time I talked to you there was some HOT guy you had a date with and two days later you wouldn't remember his name! There were just too many!"

"Well, not the case anymore, and thank God, I think I've learned a lot from those experiences! Mainly what I don't want! If my instincts are right, this guy is exactly the kind of man I've wished I could marry all of my life!

In fact, that is why were going to be a little late."

"What, you're getting married!"

"Mom, be serious! He had a gorgeous wreath delivered to my house with a sweet note and I want to drop a thank you note off by his house. I don't want to call him at work.....Do you think that would be all right?"

"I think that would be lovely." And, I have a couple of appointments this afternoon to show some homes and Christmas gifts to wrap so, if I'm not here when you get here, just get that key from under the flower pot on the porch, and Avery, please drive the speed limit and be careful......in more ways than one!"

"Got ya! Oh, Mom, are you going to get to come home with me and help me unpack?"

"You bet! I can't wait to see your new furniture and the remodel."

"Great! Ok, I'll see you as soon as we get there. Mom, I can't wait to get home, I love you."

"I love you too baby. See you soon."

Jimmie hung up the phone with lifted spirits. Avery sounded more like her old self. Something she had not heard in Avery's voice for sometime now, happiness and excitement. She had been so worried about Avery being alone since the divorce. It was not that Avery wasn't capable, or financially stable, but Bill and Jimmie knew that all Avery had ever wanted was a family of her own. It was important to Avery, and she had so much love to give.

Every night before going to sleep, Bill and Jimmie would pray for their daughter, that God would send a special man to her. A man who could give her the love she deserved and one that would appreciate her love for him. They prayed for someone who could love her children as his own. Looking upward, she said, "Thank you, God!" *I am so glad that Avery is at least going to date again. I didn't want her to be alone and down on men the rest of her life. I do hope she is careful, gee, that guy could be a serial killer for all she knows about him!* Jimmie shook her head at her last thought; *however, I hope she doesn't really get her hopes too high; this guy is probably not the kind of person she thinks he is after one blind date! Oh, well, Avery is a good judge of character, she will figure him out in a hurry.*

I just hope she isn't too critical! I know our prayers are heard. I'm not going to worry about it any more, this man may be the answer.

It was good to be going home for Christmas. Avery and the boys hadn't been home since before the divorce. They enjoyed the three hour trip home; the boys, because their mother hooked up the small TV/VCR in the car so they could watch movies in the car and Avery, because the Louisiana scenery was so beautiful going North. She loved the rolling hills dotted with graceful trees dripping with gray moss. Enormous live oak trees spread their branches as if to touch the ground. She loved the rows and rows of graceful pecan trees lined perfectly in their orchards.

Avery would dream of building a home on one of the hillsides over looking the river that ran through the valley someday. Or, maybe someday, she would purchase one of the old ante-bellam plantations near by, like the old Stanton Hall, just outside of Natchez. Each time Avery passed the lovely Civil War mansion on the way to St. Charles she would slow down and remember the story she had read in a book about Stanton Hall. It was told that a man named Fredrick Stanton built his wonderful plantation home in the mid 1800s and called it Belfast, in memory of his childhood home in Ireland. Avery would imagine herself leaning with her back against one of the graceful round columns that supported the balcony over the massive front porch of the home.

She would be wearing one of Vivian Leigh's gowns from "Gone With the Wind" and her hair would be pulled back from her face and long enough to reach all the way down her back to her waist. Of course, young suitors sipping on lemonades would surround her asking her for dances at the up coming ball. She would be charming, naturally, and cheerful as she imagined herself teasing the young men while swinging the full skirts of her gown back and forth, oh, so casually.

Each time she drove past the plantation she couldn't help but become a little saddened at the thought of how the builder and designer of this lovely old home had died only a few months after Belfast was completed. *How very sad to achieve your dream, only to have to leave it so soon!*

The escape from reality was very brief, but it was a dream that Avery never tired of. It was nice to have those dreams, she needed them every once in a while, especially now. Being a single mother of two boys was a mental, physical, and financial challenge. At least Avery was able to keep the boys in private school. She had been awarded a comfortable amount of alimony for the next three years and she wasn't planning to get a job until Jason started first grade, nearly a year from now.

Christmas was wonderful with the family at the Lynch home. Jimmie and Bill had invited all the aunts, uncles, cousins, and of course the Lynch girls and their families.

Christmas dinner consisted of flank steak stuffed with wild rice dressing, mushroom and white wine gravy, green bean bundles with lots of melted brown sugar and butter, a sweet potato casserole, spinach salad with oranges and pecans drenched with raspberry dressing, pecan pie, pralines, beautifully decorated Christmas cookies, and of course the birthday cake for the baby Jesus.

Jimmie loved to entertain and the girls all loved helping in the kitchen. It was a treasured time when only the "girls" got to be alone together while the men watched TV in the family room. They chatted and teased each other about the cottage cheese forming on their thighs. Liza and Piper teased Avery about her fairly new boob job. "Boy, Peter sure made and investment in your future when he paid for those!" Liza poked at a boob with her finger.

"Oh, you mean the twins?" Avery giggled. "Well, I thought they would help on the home scene, but *that* idea was fruitless!"

Piper, the youngest and smallest of the three Lynch girls piped in, "If I had to carry *those* twins around, you would have to be in a wheel chair!"

"Avery, have you told your sisters that you are getting married?" Jimmie smiled as she peered over her glasses at Avery while peeling potatoes.

"WHAT!" Both sisters gasp at once!

Avery laughed, "Yep, night before last, I met the man I'm going to marry, he is absolutely wonderful!"

"Flee, Satan! You lie!" Piper screamed, as the shock of Avery's statement sent her into disbelief.

"Well, kind of but, I did have a blind date last night with a heart surgeon whose wife cheated on him too. He really was a doll! We had a great time together and he has invited me to dinner when I get back home."

"Mom, you're going back with Avery today, check him out and let us know if we need to come down there and give him the sister test. I bet we will have to don't you, Liza?" Piper asked her sister with a sinister grin on her pretty face.

"Hey, wait a minute! Come to think of it, I may have to break up with him already. He was suppose to call me and I haven't heard from him yet."

Avery said, laughing. "Just think, it would be the easiest break up in history, he doesn't even have to know about it. Ha! I wouldn't have to call or anything! I'd just do it." Avery strutted around the kitchen like an important rap star.

"Sounds painless to me," added Liza. "Maybe you should before you get all mixed up in something you aren't looking for, but if you decide to keep him, be sure to let us know."

"You'll be the first!"

Grant had his boys for the first part of the Christmas vacation this year.

They shopped, went out to dinner every night and saw every new movie that was rated PG. He was supposed to take them to their mother at noon on Christmas day, and since Tara's birthday was on Christmas day, he and the boys decided to invite her over and have her spend the day with them. Grant hoped they could get through the day without a scene, but he thought it would be nice for the boys to have the family together for Christmas again.

Even after being divorced for two years, Tara still expected Grant to cater to her. In her mind Grant was hers to control. It didn't matter that she and her tennis pro were still seeing each other; it had been 5 years now, off and on. She still expected Grant to do anything she wanted him to do, and he usually did. He hated confrontation and felt that life would be easier for the boys if he just humored her, especially since they were the brunt of her rages most of the time now.

The day went fairly well. The birthday girl reveled in the attention and the boys loved having their parents together for the day. Even though Grant wanted to stay friends with his ex-wife for the boy's sakes, he felt a little uneasy, like he shouldn't be where he was.

The time seemed to drag by. At six o'clock, Tara and the boys left the house and Grant went directly to the phone. He felt a little excitement as he dialed Avery's cell phone.

"Hello"

"Hello, beautiful girl, how was Christmas at your parents?"

"Great as usual. My Mother came home with me to help get this house in order. How was your holiday?"

"It was fine, the boys wanted us to spend the day with their mother since it was her birthday, and they have gone now. Your mother is there with you?"

"Yes, she came home with me. We've been working on this house all day!"

"I was hoping I could take you to dinner tomorrow night. Would your mother like to go with us?"

"I'd love to go to dinner with you and that is so nice of you to include my mother, I'll ask her"...Jimmie was shaking her head no in the background.

"Mom says she doesn't want to go to dinner, she has tons to do, why don't you come over a little early and we can have a glass of wine with her, she would love that."

"Sounds wonderful, I'll see you around 6:30, would that be OK?"

"That's fine, I'll see you then."

Grant arrived at Avery's house promptly at 6:30. Avery and Jimmie had worked like dogs all day to get the house a little presentable.

Grant brought a bottle of wine and Jimmie and Grant chatted in the living room while Avery poured wine in real wine glasses for the three of them in the kitchen.

Avery and Jimmie talked about tennis and the teams they played on.

Grant mentioned that he had played a little tennis but didn't really get into it much. Avery and Jimmie both agreed that too many people took the game much too seriously! Jimmie asked Grant about his children and his work.

Grant was thinking, *wouldn't just know; I meet a girl I like and damned if she isn't a tennis player. Wonder if she has a thing for her pro like my ex does?* Grant couldn't help feel the bitterness for his ex wife and her lover.

"It was very nice to meet you Jimmie, are you sure you don't want to go with us?" Grant asked.

"Yes, I'm sure, I really want to get to bed early tonight. I'm pretty pooped from the holidays. You kids go on and have a great time, Thanks for asking, though."

Jimmie liked Grant. He had made a very good first impression. He seemed much more down to earth than Jimmie had expected and obviously loved children from parts of their conversation. He was calm and natural with a confident, yet humble air about him.

Grant took Avery to his house where he parked the car in the Garage. He gave her a quick tour of his home and fixed her a glass of wine. *My God, I forgot how much fun and how easy to talk to she is,* he thought. After touring the house they sat in the family room in front of the massive rock fireplace and talked. "I bought this house about a year ago directly from the contractor that was building it. I fell in love with it the first time I saw it." Grant explained. "It's a beautiful home, I can see how you fell in love!"

The tall ceilings and 9' wooden doors gave ire of old world elegance to the new, two- story, brick home. Grant had been thrilled to find a home in the center of Baton Rouge by the Baton Rouge Country Club. The location was perfect for Grant with the hospitals close by and the clinic just a few blocks away.

"I thought we would walk to the restaurant, our reservations are for 8:00.

Are you ready?" Grant asked.

"The walk sounds wonderful, I am starving!"

Avery and Grant enjoyed the walk and the meal was perfect. They decided to order Smoked Salmon and split the meal. The more they talked, the more they found they had in common. Avery talked about her divorce from Peter and problems with their marriage. Grant told Avery how Tara had cheated on him with her tennis pro and how hard she was to get along with. They both agreed that the ex-husband and ex-wife probably did each of them a favor, if the truth were known. Avery was impressed that Grant showed a sensitive side to his personality and he was such a gentleman! Grant decided not to worry about the tennis thing, even though he had vowed never to date another tennis player. He wouldn't worry just yet, anyway.

Grant had never brought a woman he was dating to meet his sons,

Therefore, he was shocked at hearing himself ask Avery if she would like to bring her boys over New Year's Eve to celebrate with him and his sons. He started to squirm a little at the thought of introducing a woman to them, but Avery seemed thrilled but explained to Grant that she had already promised that she would go to another party New Years Eve but she would love for him to come with her. They could stay for a short time at the party and then celebrate the New Year together with all of their children.

This would be the perfect out for Grant, but he surprised himself again by telling her that he had a baby-sitter for earlier in the evening; that she should bring her children over with his sitter until they got back from the party.

Damn, I just can't seem to shut my mouth! Grant thought.

"How nice, and what a great idea!" Avery smiled up at Grant and he felt himself melt at her smile.

The walk home was very romantic; Grant held Avery's hand as they walked the few blocks back to Grant's home. They didn't talk much, but they stole glances and smiled at each other. They were both happy to be where they were at that very moment.

As they entered the house, Grant helped Avery take off her coat and they both stood by the fireplace to warm their backsides. After a few moments,

Avery turned to face the fireplace and warm her hands. "I need to get home... I had a wonderful time, Grant, thank you so much for the marvelous dinner."

Grant tried to hide the disappointment he felt at her leaving. He took her hand and walked with her to the chair he had thrown her coat over. As she reached for her coat, he put his arms around her and pulled her close. They kissed long and hard. Grant kissed her as if all the loneliness and longing he had hidden for the past two years was exploding from the very depths of him. Avery found herself to be weak and trembling at his touch. She felt herself melting into his arms and reeling into semi - consciousness. Fear seized Avery and she pulled away from him, both breathing heavy.

"Stay with me tonight?" Grant begged with lingering passion.

"I can't," Avery said breathless, and then to lighten the moment she teased,

"You, are a pervert!" as she gently pushed him back by his chest and laughed.

"I really have to go, Grant. "We hardly know each other." She started putting on her coat. Would you mind taking me home now?"

"Of course not", he said in a rather raspy voice. Your mother may get worried. Can you believe it's nearly two o'clock!

The drive home was more talk about the things they had in common. Avery told Grant she was Catholic and asked if he went to church. She was thrilled to learn that he was Episcopalian and that he went to church regularly when he wasn't on call. Grant knew that the Catholic and Episcopal churches were very similar. Avery told him that she loved being Catholic because it was such a holy church wrapped in tradition, much like his church. She asked Grant if he knew what the differences in the two churches really were.

"I think the main differences are that in order to remarry in the Catholic Church you have to have your first marriage annulled. You don't have to in the Episcopal Church. And we don't believe in confession the way Catholics do. Avery, are you going to have your marriage annulled?"

"No, actually, I don't believe in annulments either. God knows I was married for eleven years and have two children by Peter. I really don't understand that church law." Avery laughed, "I don't think God would believe me if I told him I wasn't really married to that guy"

Too soon they pulled into Avery's driveway.

"Thank you Grant, I really, really had a great time." He walked her to the door and pulled her close to kiss her once more. This time, the kisses were much softer, sweeter kisses.

They stood on her porch and kissing and caressing. The soft movements of their bodies touching made them aware of only each other. The neither cold night air or chilling breeze fazed them, Avery was comfortable and warm in Grant's arms. They were unaware of any thing or anyone around until at last the bright lights of a car turning into the driveway next-door spotlighted them and broke the spell.

"Will you call me before New Years Eve? I have attention deficit disorder; I have to have lots of attention! Avery smiled at Grant as she opened the door to her house.

"Sure", he said in a rather husky voice. "I'll call and we can get our plans together for the party." He had a hard time composing himself. "Good night, Avery."

The next morning Avery staggered into the kitchen in her long terry bathrobe. Usually she dressed first, but this was a weekend and she didn't have a single thing she had to do except visit with her mother and keep finding places to put the things they unpacked.

She poured her first cup of steaming coffee and went into the office to check her e-mail. The house still seemed strangely quiet when the boys were at their dads.

Good, I've got mail....gljclinic, this must be Grant. Avery's heart quickened as she opened the e-mail.

From: gljclinic
To: Avery @aol.com

Hi beautiful. Thank you for a wonderful evening. I've been thinking of you.

Grant

Avery was thrilled at the sweet but simple gesture. *Wow, he is really something. He knows how to get to my heart!*

From: Avery

To: gljclinic@aol.com
Hello, handsome. I had a great time too. Thank you for the wonderful meal, the great company and the sweet note!

Love, Avery

CHAPTER 4

Grant left Avery's house a happy man. He felt like a teenager wanting to run, jump and click his heels together. Instead he smiled all the way home. The next day at work he told his friend and nurse, Maggie, what a great time he had with Avery.

"I'm a little worried about one thing, though," he confided.

"What's that Doctor?"

"I asked her to stay the night after only two dates. Do you think that was too.......ugh.....horny of me?'

"Pretty horny." Maggie said, "What did she say?"

"She called me a pervert."

"I guess that means she turned you down, didn't she?"

"Yes, I think calling me a pervert should have been a big turn off, don't you?"

"Well she must be a pretty nice girl. Did it turn you off?"

'No, just put me in my place, I think she is a nice girl too."

Grant waited until two days before New Years Eve to call Avery again. He had e-mailed her a note telling her how much he enjoyed their date but he was a little embarrassed about asking her to stay the night on their last date. He usually wasn't the kind of guy to hop into bed with someone so soon. He didn't know what came over him. He did know one thing for sure. He couldn't get her out of his mind and he couldn't wait to see her again. Grant thought, *This time, I will control myself. After all, I am the guy who rarely does anything spontaneous; at least I never used to do anything spontaneous. Did I?*

Avery drove her car to Grant's house on New Years Eve. She was terribly excited about the evening. Her boys were a little nervous about staying with some kids they didn't know, but they were willing to give it a try. Avery brought some sparkling grape juice for their midnight celebration drink and some disposable cameras for the kids to take pictures of each other. *I hope his kids are OK with this,* Avery thought.

Grant met them at the car and helped Avery carry her sack in and sat it on the marble counter tops in his kitchen. He introduced Travis and Trent to Hunter and Jason and then, introduced the sitter. He poured a glass of Chablis for Avery and himself. They talked and smiled at each other while watching the boys get aquatinted. Grant was still a little apprehensive about having them over, but his boys didn't seem to mind. They were excited about having their own New Year's Eve party, even if it meant sharing their dad with these strangers. He was also a little worried about what Avery though of him, now. "Avery, I want you to know that I am a little more than embarrassed about asking you to stay the other night. I'm sorry I did that. I didn't mean to ask you that."

"Actually, I took it as a compliment, and now you say you didn't *mean* it?" Avery laughed, teasing. "Gee, thanks!"

"Well, I mean I'm usually not that forward. Maybe I *am* a pervert where you are concerned." Grant looked in her eyes and smiled back at her. Avery felt a very strong attraction to him; she loved his kind eyes and perfect smile.

As soon as the boys got acquainted and started playing video games, Grant and Avery left for the party. Grant couldn't keep his eyes off Avery. She was beautiful and chic in a little black cocktail dress.

Jim Kramer, Grant's partner at the heart clinic, and his wife Julie were at the party, as well as several other people Grant knew. It seemed strange that Grant and Avery had so many of the same friends yet, had never met each other before. It didn't really matter to Grant who was or was not there. He only had eyes for one person.

Avery had been talking to a small group when she realized that Grant had wondered off. She glanced around the room and saw him standing in the doorway of a small sunroom off of the great room. He was motioning for her to come. When she got closer, he said, "Come in here, I really need to show you something."

Avery cautiously entered the room holding her wine glass to see what Grant had to show her.

"What is it", she asked

"It's this," he said softly as he guided her into his arms, taking her glass and sitting it on the table.

"He kissed her sweetly, and gently, over and over again. They lost all notice that anyone might be around.

A strict Catholic upbringing had given Avery a high since of moral character, but she was a very sensual woman and appreciated the attention. She adored the fact that Grant was so into her and responded to him with an uncharacteristic abandonment.

"Hey, you lovebirds! I didn't mean to intrude." Grant's partner Jim walked into the room just in time to catch the two in a passionate kiss. Avery turned and knocked the wine glass off of the couch table where Grant had placed it. Avery couldn't control the heat rising from her neck up her cheeks and forehead.

"Let me clean that up, I tend to be a klutz sometimes!" Avery giggled having been caught and nervously started cleaning the wine spill with the cocktail napkin that had been wrapped around the stem of the glass. Grant laughed and winked at Avery as they both bent over to pick up the glass.

"I came in to tell you lovebirds that It's only bout 30 minutes before midnight and you have to join the real world of the old married couples, so come pick out your party hats and noise makers." Jim smiled and walked out of the sunroom.

"We better get to the REAL New Year's Eve party soon, or we might not be able to." whispered Grant.

Avery giggled and they went to get her coat and to thank the host and hostess of the party. The "lovebirds" laughed all the way to Grant's house about being caught. Once there, Grant paid the baby sitter and dismissed him. Then to Avery's delight, Grant began pulling out sacks that contained silly string, noise- makers, beads, hats, and confetti from under the kitchen counter. He ran chasing all four boys with silly string. The boys threw nurf balls at Grant. They ran through the hall and slid into base under the Baby Grand piano. Avery snapped pictures and laughed at their antics.

At midnight, they poured the boys and themselves a glass of sparkling grape juice, toasted to the New Year and sang "Old Aung Zion" to the big bands on TV.

Jimmie heard the phone ringing. She raised her head off the pillow to see the alarm clock. It was only 12:30 A.M. She had not been in bed long. She and Bill had gone to their old friend's home to celebrate the New Year with several other couples. Theirs had been a calm evening sitting out side on Dee and Danielle's deck that overlooked the city lights. Their home was a modern architecture surrounded by thick trees and lovely gardens. The home and grounds were beautiful, but the stunning thing about this home was the spectacular view.

Bill and Jimmie had spent many evenings with Dee and Danielle. They had been friends since high school and had raised their children together. They vacationed together and were still the best of friends after all these years. At midnight, they donned party hats, paper glasses and blew horns and after the New Year hugs and kisses, they had come home and were already nearly asleep.

"Hello."

"Happy New Year, Mom! I'm on my way home from Grant's house. We just had the most incredible night! I just called to tell you that I *am* definitely going to marry him!"

"Happy New Year to you too, baby. So you really had fun, huh?"

"The most fun I've had in ages! Mom, he adores kids and actually plays with them himself! He is not at all a stuffy old grouch, like Peter!"

"That sounds great, Avery. Did the boys like him too?"

"They LOVED him! And, his boys are darling. We all had so much fun together!"

"Wow, he sounds like a fun guy."

"Mom, he is WONDERFUL!"

Grant let the boys sleep late Tuesday morning. He loved his quiet time in the early mornings. He sat at his computer with a cup of black coffee while he answered his e-mail. Most of the mail was from the clinic and the hospitals with scheduling questions. Then he took a minute to write Avery and tell her how much fun he and the boys had with her, Hunter and Jason last night. He had never been with anyone that he felt he could completely be himself. She was so easy to be with, so beautiful and so very much fun! He felt a little twang of loneliness at the thought of her.

After the boys woke up, Grant took them to breakfast at the Waffle House and then to an early movie. There wasn't much traffic on New Year's Day. and, in a town the size of Baton Rouge, there were always a few places open on a holiday. At 5:00 Grant took the boys back to their mother. They couldn't wait to tell their mother how much fun they had last night at their very own New Year's party!

Grant had not gotten to his drive- way until his cell phone started ringing.

"Hello."

"What in the hell are you doing to my children?" Tara screamed at Grant "Tara, calm down. What are you talking about?"

"How dare you to subject my children to one of your sleazy whores!"

"Look, Tara, Avery is not like that. She is a very nice person and the kids loved her. We just had fun."

"Don't give me that crap! I will not have you subjecting my children to a string of women! You promised me you would not bring women around the children when you have them! You will not have a woman around my children again! How dare you care so little about their feelings! Do you hear me Grant Jones?, Never again!"

Grant hung up the phone and turned it off to keep her from calling back. It had been two years sense the divorce and Avery was the first and only woman he had invited to meet his sons. He had a sick feeling in his gut. Why in the hell did he let Tara get to him the way she did! *Was I wrong to have brought Avery around the kids? She is the only woman I've dated that I thought there could be a future with. Am I supposed to get married before I introduce the boys to their new stepmother? Tara is probably yelling at the kids for having a good time at my house last night. Damn, I wish she wouldn't take her frustration out on them! I should have tried to get the boys in the divorce but damn, I hated to disrupt their little lives anymore than I had to.*

Grant walked in the house and lay down on his bed. The conversation with Tara had depressed him terribly. He fell asleep and didn't wake up until 6:00 the next morning.

From: gljclinic
To: <averyl@aol.com>
Sent: Wednesday, January 2, 2002 6:29 AM

Hi beautiful girl, I've been thinking of you. Trent told me that his basketball team and Hunter's team are playing against each other next Monday night. Trent is a really good basketball player. How about Hunter? That will be an exciting game with the two of us on opposite sides of the gym, huh?

I find myself missing having you around this morning, how would you like to meet me for lunch today? I'll call you later this morning. I need to get to work. I have a minor procedure to do this morning but I'll be finished in time for lunch.

Signed: Grant

Avery was excited after reading her e-mail. Lunch with Grant would be fun but she would have to cancel with Janie. *I'll call Janie and see If she can meet me after lunch, she will want me to go and we can meet for coffee. I'll fill her in on what has been going on with us.* Avery smiled thinking about how Janie had been dying to know all about her new love life.

Grant looked a little different today. A little younger and a little more care free. He had always had a suit and tie on when they had been together before. Grant carried himself very well. His tall and straight posture gave him the look of a confident man and he always looked wonderful in a suit, but today he looked charming: kind of little boyish, and much more approachable in the green surgical scrubs.

"Hi", Avery smiled as she scooted into the booth where Grant was scouring a menu.

"Hi, glad you could make it. You look beautiful, as usual."

"And you look great in scrubs!'

"Sure I do, the green giant, ha!"

"More like the cute intern, to me."

"Oh, so you like interns, do you?"

"Sure, they become nice doctors, like you."

Grant couldn't help but smile at Avery, she made him feel good.

"Hey, they have a great cob salad here, are you hungry?"

"Sounds great, I'm starving! I'll have that. Is that what you are having?"

"Yea, what do you want to drink?"

"Water with lemon, please; sooooo, Trent is a pretty good basketball player, huh?'

"Yea, I'd say great for his age. How about Hunter?'

"He is pretty good himself. You know what would be fun?'

"I'm listening," Grant smiled at Avery.

"Hunter has been bugging me to take him to the gym so he can practice for the big game. Why don't you, Travis and Trent meet us Sunday afternoon and we'll all play."

Grant loved the idea and loved the fact that Avery wanted to play with the children.

"That's a great idea, I'm sure the boys will want to come. Let's make it a date!"

Grant kissed Avery on the cheek in the parking lot when they left the restaurant. Grant told Avery, "I have the boys this weekend, so I'll call you when I get a chance."

It was a stroke of luck that Avery and Grant had the children for their parental visitation weekends at the same time. Avery knew that Peter certainly wouldn't change weekends to accommodate her. He was angry that Avery was dating. He threatened to take her back to court to get the children because he felt she had gotten too many baby-sitters during the holidays. He continued to call her every day and usually an argument ensued. He expected her to stay home with the children and he was frustrated at losing control of her. It was a hard pill for Peter to swallow.

Avery, Hunter, and Jason were excited about taking Trent, Travis and Grant on in a basketball game. Avery planned to cheat with every move she made on Grant. Fouling him would really be fun! They had not seen each other since lunch Wednesday, although they had spoken often over the phone and exchanged e-mail several times a day between Grant's patients. A lot of their conversations included jibes and teasing about the big game on Sunday.

Sunday morning before Avery and the boys left for church, Grant called.

"Hi, beautiful girl."

"Hey, Michael Jordan!" Avery teased.

"Uh, that's why I called, Avery, I think maybe we should take a rain check on the basketball game."

"Oh, is someone sick?" asked Avery, concerned.

"No, I have been just thinking. It's probably too soon for us to start getting the children together just yet."

"Oh, uh, well, OK, I understand." Avery tried to hide her disappointment. "We'll just have to whip you guys another time then."

"Thank you for understanding, Avery."

"Grant, I want to protect my children and I'm sure you want to protect yours. I understand. Listen, we are walking out the door for church so I have to run. Thanks for calling."

Avery was crushed. She wanted so badly to really understand, but it was so hard to, even though she told Grant that she did. *Why would he seem so excited all week and then at the last minute cancel? Why did he have us over to meet his kids New Year's Eve if he was that protective of his sons? I hope I haven't made a mistake by getting involved with him. I wonder if there is something about him that I'm not seeing.*

Monday rolled around quickly. Christmas vacation was over for the children and the painters and carpenters filed in and out of Avery's house all day. After school Avery sat with the boys at the kitchen table to help with homework and stuck some frozen chicken strips in the oven, mixed up a green salad and put some frozen, fried potatoes in the broiler for supper. Just when they were finishing dinner, the phone rang.

"Hey, you guys ready for the big game?" Grant asked Avery.

"Yea, we are there!"

"Well, I don't know if I will be able to come, I'm on call, but I'll try."

"Hope you can. I guess we will be sitting on opposite sides, Huh."

"Guess so!" Grant laughed. "Avery, I'm off call tomorrow, how about going to dinner?"

"I'll see if I can get a sitter, and let you know, OK?"

"Great! I better run now, talk to you later."

"Bye, thanks for calling." Avery had been feeling a little cautious about Grant ever since he cancelled their basketball practice date with the children Sunday. *I wonder if Grant is nervous to be seen with me in public? I wonder if that is why he may not come to the game. I wonder if he still has a thing for his ex-wife? Maybe he doesn't want her to see us together. Hmmm. Maybe I just won't go to dinner with him, I may need to cool this thing off with him.* Avery was feeling a more than a little unsure of herself.

The basketball gym was crowded and smelled a little rank, like it had been in constant use by sweaty little boy bodies. Five year old Jason had decided to wear his LSU "Tigers" basketball uniform to watch the game. That was a treacherous thing to do since Trent's team was called "The Tigers", and Jason's big brother, Hunter's team was called the

Dragons! Hunter and Avery both tried to get Jason to change his clothes, but Jason would have none of it.

"I want to woot for Mr. Gwant and Twent!" Avery scanned the gym and saw that Peter and his parents, sister and her children were all there for the big game.

"Mom, I need a coke, pleeeease?" Jason begged his mom as they were walking through the gym to the bleachers where they would sit.

"Jason, wait till half time. You just ate supper and you will want something then."

"But, Mom, I'm thiwsty!"

"Run get a drink out of the water fountain, Jason. You have to wait for your coke."

"OhhhhhhK." Jason gave in.

After Jason and Avery secured their seats in the bleachers on the Dragon side of the gym, Avery skimmed the opposite side for Grant, but she didn't see him. She spent the first half of the game filming it with her movie camera. At one point she stood up and went to the wall under the goal to get a better shot. She felt something hit her legs from behind and felt her knees bend involuntarily from under her. She turned expecting to see Jason behind her. Peter was standing in the narrow space between her and the wall of the gym with a grin on his face.

"Peter, I thought you were Jason." *I guess that is how he flirts with all of the other women!* She thought to herself while she tried to hide her embarrassment by his familiarity.

Avery moved away from Peter and filmed a few more seconds before she went back up into the stands to sit by Jason.

Half time came in a hurry. The "Tigers" were ahead by five points. It had been a really exciting game and the eight year olds had played hard.

Jason immediately started pulling on his mother's hand to take him to the concession stand. As mother and son headed for the door, Avery noticed Grant had made it to the game in his green scrubs and was standing against the gym wall in "Tiger" territory right by the door she had to go through. She also noticed that he was watching her. *I have to walk right past him to get to the concession stand. Do I stop and talk to him? Would Peter and his family have a stroke if I do. His ex-wife must be here too. I wish I didn't feel so weird about just going over to talk to him.*

"Mawom, come on!!!!" Jason tugged at his mother's hand to go.

"OK, OK!" as they reached to door, Avery looked at Grant and smiled. He smiled back as Jason ignored the world around him and continued to drag his mother by the hand into the hall and to the line of children and parents at the concession stand counter.

Avery was standing in line, talking to some of the parents of the "Dragons" when she felt a tap on her shoulder. She turned to see Grant's ex-wife with eleven-year-old Travis standing in front of her. Her hands were on his shoulders as if she had been guiding him.

"Hello, Avery." Tara's look was stern.

"Hello, Tara, I haven't seen you since we worked together on that Holiday House committee for Junior League." Avery was a little taken back by Tara's approach.

I'm surprised she remembers me, I hardly know her. I hope we can be friends.

"I heard that you have met my sons."

"Yes, I have, and they are great kids." Avery said, smiling down at Travis. Travis was smiling broadly at Avery.

"Well, how very nice for you; I don't expect you to see them ever again, is that clear, you just stay away from my children!" Tara blurted out at Avery, then turned and pushed Travis in front of her, back into the crowded gym.

Avery felt the heat rise in her face. She was humiliated and angry. *How dare she be so hateful to me, and in front of Travis! The poor child must be terribly embarrassed! My God, I called Peter's girlfriend to tell her that I hoped we could be friends. I actually told her that I blamed Peter for breaking up our marriage, not her. After all, if she is going to be the stepmother of my children, I want to be on decent terms with her. Poor Grant, his children don't need that kind of pressure. Travis will be afraid to see me again. What a Bitch!!!!!*

"What was that all about?" asked Mary Beth.

Mary Beth and her husband, Nick, had been good friends with Avery and Peter for years. They were devastated by their friend's divorce and had helped them both through it. Mary Beth had been wonderful to take Hunter and Jason home after school to play with her children during some of the counseling sessions and attorney appointments, and now, Mary Beth and Nick managed to be friends with both Avery and Peter by not taking sides.

"I have had a few dates with her ex-husband, and evidently, she doesn't like it."

"With Grant? Oh, Avery, he is so nice. I'm so glad you are going out with him. I did hear that she was hoping for reconciliation. That's strange though, I also heard that she is still dating Ragon, her tennis pro, and that she was definitely the cause of her marriage breaking up. I think she just wants her cake and eat it too, Avery, don't let her get to you that is exactly what she wants; to run you off!"

Beth was so wonderful. She was always there for Avery and always kind and accepting. Jason and Avery walked coolly back into the gym. Avery didn't look at Grant; she couldn't face him right now.

The second half was a re-run of the first, back and forth with the lead of the score. The little boys ran up and down the court playing with all their hearts. Avery couldn't seem to get back into it. She watched Tara and Grant from across the gym; Tara, in the bleachers sitting with Travis, pretending to be watching the game with her hand to her mouth. Then she would catch a glimpse of Grant, standing against the wall, with one leg bent and his foot against the wall. When she caught him looking at her, she looked away. Her smile was gone. She decided not to tell Grant what had happened between her and Tara. She didn't want to cause any more trouble.

After the game, Avery hung back in the gym talking to other parents of the defeated Dragons. She was hoping that Peter, his family and Tara would be gone before she had to walk back out to the concession area and parking lot. She was even hoping that Grant would be gone. When she realized that she was one of the few people still in the gym, she gathered her children and headed for the door. To her surprise, Grant was there waiting in the door way for her.

"Some game, huh?" Grant put his hand on Hunters sweaty head and ruffled his hair.

"Great game, except the wrong team won!" Avery tried to sound upbeat.

Jason ran up to Grant and threw his arms around his legs.

"Hey little man," Grant put his hand on Jason's back to keep him from falling backwards as he looked up in adoration at Grant. Then Jason hopped off and ran with Hunter out of the door to the car. Grant and Avery walked behind them.

"Did you find a sitter for tomorrow night?"

"I haven't yet, but I will call Christine and see if she can come."

"Wonderful, I'm looking forward to it. I have made reservations at Starkys. It's a really good place, tons of atmosphere."

"That sounds nice." Avery smiled up at Grant as she reached her car.

"I'll pick you up around 7:00, unless I hear from you, OK?"

"Yes, that will be great."

I just wonder what he would have said if I had told him what Tara had done? I think she had a big hand in the reason Grant cancelled our basketball practice together. Poor Grant, she must be giving him a hard time about us dating. Well, I refuse to let that ole bitty run me off so easily!" Avery immediately went home and secured Christine to baby-sit for her tomorrow evening.

Grant had been able to slip away from the hospital long enough to see most of his son's basketball game. He had been standing against the gym wall in case he had to leave quickly, watching the game catching glimpses of Avery. She was so lovely inside and out. He had watched her hold a friend's baby and help a small retarded boy climb to the top of the bleachers. He had watched her film parts of the game. He was watching her walk with Jason back to the bleachers for the second half of the game when his cell phone went off. *Uh, oh, Mr. Harris might be having some problems.* "Hello."

"Grant, I just ran into your sleazy girlfriend!" *What in the hell is she doing here? Can't you keep her away from you and my children even for one ballgame? Do you have any idea how totally embarrassed I am to be in the same gym as her? You have never used very good judgment, but this is ridiculous! Don't you think your children are humiliated to have to see her here at Trent's ballgame while I am sitting right here?!"*

"Tara, Avery is here because her son pl..." Tara hung up on Grant before he could finish his statement. *Oh, I really think she is THE DEVIL! Grant felt his blood pressure rise.* His phone rang again. This time Grant looked at the display on his phone and saw that it was Tara's cell number showing on his caller ID. He didn't answer the phone nor, did he look up at Tara in the stands. When Tara left the gym she stormed past Grant with Travis and Trent close behind her.

Grant playfully grabbed at his sons and ruffled their hair, telling Trent what a great game he had played. The boys giggled and playfully wrestled around with their father for a second until they caught the evil eye of their mother stopped at the exit door waiting for them. They gave their dad a knowing look and he gave them a wink as they ran out of the door, following Tara to her car.

Dinner at Starky's was all that Grant had promised. Candles, low lighting, small private dining areas and a charming martini bar. The atmosphere was quite different than that of the bawdy restaurants and bars Baton Rouge was known for. Grant and Avery sipped on French martinis before dinner. They talked about how they felt when they first met. Avery told Grant how hard she tried to get out of their date. Grant told Avery how he hated blind dates and wondered why he was so compelled to go on theirs. They wondered if it was fate or an accident that they had met. Both agreed that they were so happy they had.

In the back of Avery's mind, she couldn't help but wonder what was really going on with Grant and his ex-wife, after all, he *had* spent all of Christmas day with her. He had told her that. *Would he have told me that if there was more going on than he had revealed? Mary Beth did say that Tara wanted to get back together with Grant. I wonder. He certainly is great a hiding his feelings if he has anything for her. Hmmmmmmm.*

Their meal of white fish stuffed with crab was delectable.

After dinner Grant took Avery to his house, lit his fireplace with remote control and put on a CD of Elton John. Avery made herself comfortable on the couch. Grant went into the kitchen and returned with two glasses of Chablis.

"I've wanted to have you all to myself for what seems a very long time, Avery." Grant said in a low husky voice as he started kissing her neck.

"This is sooooo nice, Grant."

They kissed and talked and kissed. Each kiss grew a little longer and more passionate. "Where have you been my whole life, Avery? I didn't know there was anyone like you out there."

"Thank you, Grant, you are so sweet.

"I am falling for you, Avery."

"Please don't say something like that, Grant. I don't want to get hurt again."

"I know you are vulnerable, Avery, I'm afraid too."

"You know, I didn't think I would ever feel this way about anyone again." Grant whispered in her ear and kissed her between words on her neck. She turned to face his face and put her hand gently on his cheek.

Her heart ached for him. She kissed him deeply and they became lost in a swirling sea of passion. Avery felt an unfamiliar ache and a delicious heat rise from deep within her. She was oblivious to time and space. Grant felt a raw hunger for her, but it was different this time. This time, he didn't want to take from her selfishly; he wanted to give her all of his feelings, his passion, and his heart. He caressed her and enjoyed the arousal he brought to her..

Suddenly, Avery had visions of Tara at the gym last night. She pulled away and was shaking all over, "Grant, I'm so sorry, I just can't do this. I want to so badly, but I just can't!"

"Avery, its fine, believe me, I am happy. I'm very happy."

"I really hope you understand. It's just that I've never had sex with anyone I didn't marry. Ha! And I only married one guy, I guess it's the old Catholic upbringing, and there *are* some issues. Are you sure you are all right?"

"I am wonderful, Avery. Thanks to you. Let's go for a walk and cool off. I want to show you what I am thinking about doing to the house."

Grant didn't want to rush Avery. He could understand her caution and appreciated it. He couldn't help but wonder what she meant when she said there were issues. He wanted to give her time and maybe she would confide in him what her issues were besides the Catholic thing.

Thursday evening, Grant came to Avery's for dinner. She prepared a beef tender with mushroom and wine sauce with all the trimmings. Grant was impressed. Jason and Hunter were excited to be included. They were beginning to get attached to Grant, especially Jason. Hunter was a little more protective of his mother and a little more leery of having anyone around his mother except for his daddy. After dinner, Grant made himself at home and played with the boys while Avery cleaned up the kitchen. He divided his time between the computer game he brought to Hunter and the Scooby Doo movie he brought to Jason.

"Time for bed, boys; thank Mr. Grant for the great surprises he brought you and let's hop upstairs to get your P.Js. on."

"Ah, Mom, do we have too?" The boys whined in unison.

Grant grinned, pleased that the boys wanted to stay and play. "Hey, guys, come on, I'll go up with you and show you the neat trick Travis showed me how he gets the tooth paste on his tooth brush without holding the tube! "Yipee," cried little Jason, and the boys took off running for the stairs. Grant was certainly wonderful with children. Avery took mental note of every move he made with them.

Avery and Grant sat on the couch by the fireplace in her living room. She had poured them both a glass of wine and they sat arm in arm enjoying their newfound silence. The wine warmed and calmed them. They were both enjoying a new found feeling of well- being.

"I am going to visit my sister and mother next week in Georgia for a couple of days. My sister is building a new house that she wants me to see, and my grandfather is gravely ill. I'm hoping he makes it till I get there to see him."

"Oh, Grant, I am so sorry about your grandfather. At least you will enjoy the visit with your mom and sister."

"Yes, we are very close. My grandfather is my dad's father and I have not been close to that side of the family since the divorce. I really want to see them both though." That's another thing about Tara, she never wanted to visit my family."

"That makes it hard. Peter never wanted to visit mine either, and I am so close with my sisters and parents, it used to kill me that he wouldn't visit them with me, or if he did come, he would make us leave at the crack of dawn the next morning. Speaking of sisters, mine want to come meet you and go out on a date with us," Avery giggled at the thought.

"Could they come this weekend? I would love to meet them too."

"They were talking about coming this weekend. Are you sure you could handle all three of us?"

"If they are anything like you, I would be in heaven!"

More like Purgatory! In fact, it will probably be more like Hell, they are very protective of me!" Avery laughed.

"I can handle it!" Grant said softly as he kissed her on her neck.

"Grant, thank you so much for being so sweet to my boys. That means more to me than anything in the world. I really think you are the kindest, gentlest and wonderful man I have ever met. Tell me you are for real...."

"Avery, I think you are a wonderful mother, and I adore you." Grant whispered in her ear, and then he smiled a wicked little smile and asked, "Can we please go to bed soon?'

Avery laughed at him but earnestly looked him in the eyes to see his reaction. "I want to make love to you so badly, but I can't sleep with anyone unless I am sure that what we feel for each other is real. Can you understand that, Grant?"

"Yes, I do. Avery, I'm very vulnerable right now too, but I do adore you and I want to hold you; I want to have you hold me."

"Then, would you be OK if we could just cuddle?" Avery felt kind of silly asking that of Grant, after all, she was a 35-year-old woman, but she couldn't help how she felt, and no matter how uncomfortable she was at having to admit her seemingly outdated or childish convictions. To betray her beliefs that sex without love is wrong, would be an unforgivable violation to her self worth. She had done that once before and still felt the guilt.

"I would be happy and I would love to cuddle with you." Grant's sincere answer put her at ease and made her love him a little more.

"Grant, there is something bothering me." Avery knew their relationship could not go any farther until she had him answer a few questions.

"What is it, Avery?"

"Well, you know the other day when you decided to take a rain check on our basketball game; you said you thought it was too soon to get our children together. Is there a reason you feel that way?"

"Well, I guess that I was really thinking it was too soon because Tara hasn't had a chance to get used to the idea of it yet."

"Grant, please help me understand why it is so important to you what Tara thinks of you dating someone?"

Avery's heart was breaking.

"No, Avery, it's not *that*, I could care less what she thinks about me dating. It's the fact that she is a very jealous woman and will take her frustrations out on the boys. I hate that for them, but I don't really know what to do about it right now. I think that with time she will get used to the idea of another woman being around the boys. Right now she is being horrible. She calls and e-mails me every five minutes and gripes about me having you and the boys over New Years Eve. She says hateful and mean things. I really don't know what to do except to give her time to get used to the idea, not for me, but for the children."

"I'm so sorry, Grant. Maybe it would be best if I just went away, at least for a while. I've heard that she wants you back. That she is very jealous of us, and if there is the most remote possibility that you could work it out with her, it would probably be the best thing for the boys."

"Avery, please don't even think that way! I couldn't stand it if you went away."

"But, Grant, I can't stand it that I am the cause of you and the boys being hurt now. Grant, please be honest with me, is there still anything between you and Tara?" Some of her friends that I know have told me that they heard you were trying to get back together with her."

"Avery, I did try to work it out with her. It will not work. I have tried to be half way nice to her, spending Christmas day with her and not fighting with her and she builds it up that I am trying to get back with her. I assure you that I have no feelings for her except disgust. *Please,* Avery, *please* believe me; that I care very much about only you. I don't want to lose you now!"

"Does that mean that you are my boyfriend?" Avery asked, grinning up at him.

"It certainly does, you are the only girlfriend that I want."

Avery took his hand in hers as he kissed her tenderly on her neck and in her hair. "Thanks for explaining it to me. I promise I will try to be more understanding, now that I know the story. Let's go watch TV in my room." She gently pulled him off of the couch and led him, barefoot to her bedroom and they crawled on top of the bed together. They held each other for hours talking and kissing and falling in love.

Avery talked to her mother and sisters every day by phone or e-mail. Liza and Piper were anxious to meet this man that Avery talked about so much. They had been warning her not to move too quickly with this romance. They were anxious to see if he was really as nice a guy as Avery thought or was she seeing him out of need? Did he have the doctor "God" syndrome, and they were certainly going to ask him what his intentions were toward their sister!

Liza and Piper both worked with their mother in the real estate office so Jimmie was going to stay home and take care of business.

Avery and her sisters decided to pick Grant up in Avery's car and to treat him to the evening out. Liza and Piper were a little nervous on the way to his house. But as usual, when the three girls were together, they joked and had a great time. Avery was scared to death of what her sisters were going to put Grant through. She nervously laughed at everything they said. She knew neither of them would ever do nor say anything to deliberately hurt her, but she knew that they would certainly be scrutinizing every move Grant made, and that was the part that was making her nervous.

In the car on the way to Grants house, Liza said "I'm going to ask him for free birth control pills, he should make himself useful and be good for something!"

"Yea, I want a free pelvic exam! Teased Piper.

"For God sakes, he's a heart surgeon, thank goodness! Avery exclaimed.

'Oh, that's worse! Heart surgeons usually think they are smarter than anyone else. He will probably think we're all idiots. Hope he doesn't ask us what you made on your A.C.T. test in high school,

Avery, ha! He will think you slept through it!" Liza teased.

"Like you only made a point higher than I!" Avery retorted.

"Well, at least we were allowed into college." Liza had a flashback, "Oh, Piper, I recall you had to take a summer course before *you* could get in, ha!" Piper sat in the back seat frowning at Liza.

"That's OK though, I think people expect a former Miss Louisiana to be a little dumb, especially since you're blonde."

"Yea, Yea, Yea, at least I have my degree, Miss drop out of college to get married." retorted Piper.

"Don't remind me!" Liza winced

"Hey Trashery, you haven't slept with him yet, have you?" Piper changed the subject and the attention to Avery.

"Piper, If I had, you would be the last to know!" Avery and Liza laughed at their little sister. She had always been the tattletale of the family.

The girls giggled all the way to Grant's house.

Grant met the girls at the front door. The house was dimly lit with candles and a warm fire in the fireplace. Grant gave each girl a glass of Beringer Cabernet. The four sat in the living room, Avery close to Grant in a large club chair, and Liza and Piper on the couch facing them. Liza's first impression of Grant was that he was will dressed, kind of cute, well composed. He had lovely manners. He could possibly grow on her. Piper was a little more cynical. The girls looked through a photo album that was sitting on Grant's coffee table and asked him about the people in the photos.

After some small talk and a couple glasses of wine, the girls took Grant to a quaint Italian restaurant where Grant ordered them Cosmo martinis. Piper's first thought was, *I wonder if he is an alcoholic?*

Piper, the youngest and most straight-laced of the three started the inquisition.

Smiling broadly she asked Grant "Sooooo, how many martinis do you usually drink in an evening?"

"Oh, I limit myself to two. More than that and you're too stupid to know if your having fun or not."

"Avery says you love kids, would you like to have some of mine?" Liza the dry one of the bunch asked.

"Soooooo," Piper continued, would you like to have more children?"

"Well, I would love more children, I've thought about it. Maybe I'm getting to old, I don't know."

"What do you think about abortion?" Piper got right to the meat. "*Piper*, don't ask him something so personal." Avery frowned at her little sister and kicked her under the table.

"Ouch! Piper winced

"Grant, Avery turned to look him in the eyes, "We call Piper the Virgin Mary, and don't mind her."

"Well, someone in this family has to keep them my sisters on the straight and narrow!" retorted Piper, laughing.

"I don't mind answering that question at all, I love children so much that I can't agree with abortion unless of course, the pregnancy puts the mother in a life or death situation."

"Good answer, Grant!" Piper liked that one.

Liza, the oldest sister, and mother of four children was enjoying this time away from her family, and savoring every sip of her martini.

"Because you're a doctor, do you have women hanging all over you?" Liza thought she was being clever.

"Well, I don't. But if I did, I wouldn't date any of my patients, so it's fortunate for me that I have that rule since most of my female patients are over 80." They all laughed.

Grant was a perfect gentleman to the three. They had a wonderful meal and more fun as the evening progressed. As the girls dropped Grant off at his home, Piper yelled after him. "Hey, by the way, we give you and A+!"

"You girls are horrible! And I love you for it! Isn't he wonderful!" Avery smiled dreamily. She was in love and she was too far-gone even if they had not liked him.

CHAPTER 5

The sister weekend was fun, even though Avery spent most of her time talking on the phone to Grant!

On Sunday morning, the weather was wonderful and warm so the girls sat on Avery's small patio drinking coffee before church. It was nice to get away from their everyday routines and it was great to be together talking about their date last night. Avery was relieved that her sisters approved of Grant.

At 11:00, the three girls drove to the large Catholic Church down the street from Avery's house and after church; the girls went to lunch at the old "Pic-a-deli" in downtown Baton Rouge. Grant told Avery last night that he would like to see her Sunday night before he left for Georgia, so while she and her sisters were having lunch, she had them help her plan a special surprise for him.

After lunch the sisters hugged and Liza and Piper left Avery for their families in St. Charles feeling much better that Avery was in love with a guy they approved of and that she was happy. They both agreed that Grant would fit into the family nicely. On the drive home, Piper had a thought, "Oh brother, he hasn't met Dad yet, has he?" Both girls giggled at the thought.

Avery stopped off at the grocery store to pick up some fresh crawfish and stopped by the flower section to pick up a couple of rose buds and a small card. She drove to Grant's house and placed the rose on the front porch of his house with a note that read: *You are cordially invited to the home of Avery Lyons for dinner and drinks tonight at 7:00 P.M.* Avery didn't ring the doorbell to see if he was at home, she hoped he wasn't there to see her. She then called Mary Beth on her cell phone. "Hey, M.B., it's Avery. I have a favor to ask of you."

"Sure, Ave, what is it?"

"Would you mind if I could have Peter bring the kids by for you to baby-sit from around 6:00 to 9:30 and then I will pick them up? I am having Grant over for dinner, he is going out of town tomorrow morning for about a week and I would love to be alone with him for a couple of hours."

"Oh, how romantic! Do you want them to spend the night?"

"Goodness, no; it's a school night and Grant won't be able to stay late anyway, his plane leaves really early in the morning."

"Sure, I would love to help you out with this one! Have Peter drop them off, I'll be at home. Hey, I was going to call you tonight anyway. Could you pick my kids up from school tomorrow? I have a dentist appointment."

"Sure! I will be so happy to get to help _you_ out for a change, and the boys will be thrilled!"

Then, she called Peter and told him to take the children to Mary Beth's at 6:00 instead of bringing them home, and for some reason he didn't argue about it. He must not have suspected she was planning a date with Grant or he surely would have been disagreeable. She must remember to do something extra nice for Mary Beth tomorrow! She then rushed home to cook a special Italian meal of pasta and crawfish e'toufe. She sat a table for two in front of her fireplace in the living room with her finest china, crystal and silver. On Grant's plate she placed a single rose bud. She had his favorite white wine chilling, and put on her favorite C.D. of Elton John. She then jumped in the shower and emerged from her bath feeling fresh and calm. She had not talked to Grant all afternoon and started to worry that maybe he had not seen his invitation. She was lighting the fireplace in the living room when the front door bell rang.

"Hi, I was just hoping you got my invitation." Avery was all smiles as she pulled him in through the doorway.

"You are so much fun! I loved the invitation." Grant handed her the rose bud she had left on his porch. "My God, do you always look this beautiful?"

"Of course I do, especially in the mornings when my hair is matted and the make up is a' natural."

Avery could tell that Grant was really enjoying her company and the special surprise that she had dreamed up for him. He enjoyed every bite of the e'toufe and complemented her on the choice of wine. He loved the romantic dinner served in the living room. After dinner they sat on the couch next to the fireplace and enjoyed another glass of wine with Elton John. Their small talk led to sweet kisses that escalated into passion. They couldn't get enough of each other. At 9:00 Avery had to break away to go pick up the boys, and Grant to go pack.

"I am going to miss you, Avery, I love having you as my girlfriend."

"And I love having you as my boyfriend." Grant had finally met someone that suited his own personality. They had real fun together, they could be silly, and he loved that about her. In a world of stress, sickness and death, to be able to have some fun and be silly was very important to him. She was romantic, he loved that, she was fun and creative, he loved that, she laughed at herself, he loved that, and she was sexy, he really loved that, but most of all he loved what he saw in her heart. She had a pure heart, and even though she had been hurt badly, she was able to open herself up to him with an almost child-like trust. Grant knew he was falling in love.

Avery offered to take Grant to the airport early tomorrow morning for his flight to Georgia but he had told the boys that they couldn't take him since Tara would be the one to have to drive them. She probably put them up to asking him that, anyway. Nope, he didn't want to see her if he didn't have to. So, he was going to take his own car and leave it parked in the airport. "Grant leaned down to kiss Avery goodbye before leaving her house. "You be checking your e-mail, I'll write you as often as I can, OK?

"OK", Avery was sweet but a little quiet thinking of Grant being gone for a few days. "I'm going to miss you terribly." She whispered to him as they kissed again. She stood at the door and watched Grant back out of her driveway and pull out into the street. She then locked the door and left to pick up her boys.

The alarm was going off and the phone was ringing at the same time the next morning. "Hello," a sleepy Avery answered the phone. "Hey, beautiful girl, I'm on the plane."

"I didn't expect to hear from you so soon." Avery was pleased.

"I miss you already! Did you happen to tell your nosy sisters that I thought they were great? I forgot to ask you last night."

"You really think they are great after that inquisition?"

"Hell, yes, I got an A+, didn't I?"

"Yes, you passed, yea!"

"Hey, I have to run, the plane is taxiing down the runway. Bye my sweetheart girlfriend."

Avery could tell Grant was in a great mood, he must be excited to get to go home for a few days.

From: "Grant L Jones"<gljonesclinic@aol.com>
To: <Avery@aol.com>

Subject: Re: hi

Hi sweetheart girlfriend. Or would you rather I call you beautiful, you are you know. I'm still dreaming of the delicious dinner as well as the entire ambience that went with it… I am impressed with Avery's Kitchen. I really had a wonderful time. So far, last night out did any evening I have ever spent with anyone. It was all wonderful from that enticing invitation to the rose to your sweet lips. Only one thing was missing and we will get to that later. My sister and I are going out to a new martini bar tonight. I'll write you later. Thank you again for a wonderful evening! I already miss you!

Later GLJ

From: "Avery"avery@aol.com
To: "Grant L Jones"gljonesclinic@aol.com

Subject: Re: hi

I love for you to call me beautiful; I especially love for you to call me sweetheart girlfriend. I might prefer princess, though, since I have a choice, ha! (I've always wanted to be one) Glad you enjoyed our date at home. I loved you being there. You are the most wonderful man I have ever known. I think I dreamed you up out of my fairy tale books, sometimes I feel like I am on a roller coaster, flying into never-land with you, and I love it. I like my new boyfriend! I miss you too, very much! Have a great time with your sister.

Love Avery

From: "Grant L Jones"gljonesclinic@aol.com
To: Avery@aol.com

Subject: Re: hi

Hi my sexy girlfriend, beautiful princess:

How was that! I am loving it too. For me, it's more like being shot from a cannon rather than being on a roller coaster. A roller coaster ride has some ups and downs and it been all up! Speaking of which, I had a conversation with my sister, Katie last night about you; we were drinking martinis, remember? I'm not sure I will remember much, but I'll try. Anyway, she decided to analyze my situation in life right now. She said things like "You know, what comes up, must come down. And the fast burning flame burns out quickly. I think she is a little cynical because she and her boyfriend just broke up. She asked me tons of questions, like, "Do you love her? I asked her how was I supposed to know for sure? What about her past?" I told her you that you did have a thing for your tennis pro while you were separated. She nearly died laughing and said, "Boy, do you just try to pick girls that have *things* for tennis pros? She fell off her bar stool laughing and broke her hip! (not really) She wanted to know if there was anything else hidden in your closet. Not really, I made that part up too.

Actually that is not the way it happened, I made most of that up. The truth is I have a few issues that I need to work through but that does not have any affect on how much I love being with you. In fact right now, I am having a withdrawal attack… I need a quick pill packed with your kisses………..

Call you later. Love, your boyfriend

From: <Avery@aol.com>
To: gljonesclinic@aol.com

Subject: issues

Hi handsome,

I understand Katie's concern over the "tennis pro" thing. It is kind of ironic, huh? I hope you understand about that, but we can talk about it anytime you want to. I have been made to feel so dirty about that. That is one thing in my life I truly regret. On a lighter note, I had a fight with the dog today. She grabbed Jason's show and tell and ran out the door with it as I was trying to get the kids in the car for school. I chased and cursed her, but all considered, I thought I controlled myself quite nicely. Jason and Hunter laughed and said I looked wild! Maybe it was the Avery in the closet coming out! You know, she isn't so bad. Certainly no psycho. I wouldn't say she is shy, but maybe a little scared, a little insecure and a little vulnerable. She will come out and play if you ask her to. She is very honest and will answer any questions that you might have. I bet closet Avery and closet Grant will like each other (I would like to meet him too) they might even become boyfriend and girlfriend.

I read a thing that the Dali Lama said. It was that relationships based on need were no good. The thing with Brett was just that! I've been made to feel so dirty about that by Peter and his family that it is hard for me to talk about it. They told their friends that I was the one who had an affair because they just couldn't stand to have Peter take the blame for our failed marriage. It is important to me that you know the truth. It is not as interesting as gossips have made it out to be. I had been so happy in my own little housewife world. Closing out all the warnings, dismissing Peter for the Jerk he was, feeling guilty because I thought he worked all the time. I was an emotional train wreck when I found out about Peter's affair. I felt so unattractive and needy. I am sorry that I was not stronger than to run to the first open arms there were. I regret my weakness, and I regret hurting Brett. Whew! Enough of that! How are you? I miss you, Love Avery

CHAPTER 6

Fortunately, Grant had gone to see his grandfather because it was the last time he would see him again. He died while Grant was visiting in Georgia and Grant had to stay a few more days to help make funeral arrangements attend the funeral.

Avery couldn't wait to see Grant, it seemed like he had been gone forever. He was to come to her house directly from the airport.

She had been cleaning the house and was about to finish primping in her pretty, new bathroom. Avery looked around her surroundings with pride. She had just completed the decorating with a white-washed blue paint for the walls and a pale yellow ceiling to connect the pale yellow master bedroom walls adjoining the bath.

A six-foot mirror framed in pewter hanging from the ceiling to the rim of the new whirlpool bathtub added a touch of elegance and made the small bath seem much larger than it was. The master bed looked inviting with a dusty blue Indian gauze bedspread over the massive king size sleigh bed and wide, cream wooden blinds covering the window were surrounded by a dusty gauze fabric and tied in a fashionable swag in the center of the window.

The boys were already tucked in for the night and watching a movie in bed while Avery prepared for Grant's arrival.

The peace and quiet of the evening was interrupted by the phone ringing. Avery had to walk into her bedroom to answer the call; her heart raced as she expected to hear Grant's voice on the other end of the line.

"Avery?" It was Peter.

"Hi, Peter, the kids are in bed."

"I hoped they would be. Listen, I have made an appointment for us to go to a child psychologist Friday morning."

"Peter, the children seem to be doing very well, is there a special reason you think we need to do this?" Avery was concerned.

Peter's toned changed from halfway friendly to angry. "Of course there is a reason! Avery, you are not doing right by the children. Lana told me you sent them half dressed to school and with no breakfast. I called Hunter's teacher and she told me Hunter was behind in his times tables and had not read all of the books he is suppose to be reading. You are letting him fall behind in school and you don't seem to be taking care of them; Lana even told me you let Hunter stay home by himself while you went to the store! I think you are too damn selfish these days, doing just what you want to do, dating this Grant guy to care about what happens to the kids!"

"Peter, it is so easy for you to throw accusations at me. You certainly didn't seem to stop and think what you were doing to the children and me while you were out screwing every Tuesday and Thursday night, did you? I let Hunter stay home by himself for 10 whole minutes. He has been begging me to let him stay by himself because Lana lets Carrie stay by herself some. He thinks that is grown up. I have never sent the kids to school without breakfast and never sent them half dressed!" Avery was shaking with anger. The very idea that he would accuse her of being a bad mother! That was the only thing he used to say she did right!

"Are you going to come to the psychologist appointment or not?" Peter demanded in a very cold tone.

"I wouldn't miss it for the world!" Avery said and slammed down the phone.

Tears were brimming in her eyes, her throat hurt from trying to hold back her sobs of anger and hurt. *That Bastard! How dare he accuse me of putting myself before my children! How dare Lana tell Peter that I am neglecting the boys!* Avery's joy was her children. Avery thought Lana would be neutral and not take sides, *I guess that blood really is thicker than water! I will not subject the boys or myself to their speculations anymore. I'm going to call Lana in the morning and stop car-pooling with her.* Avery could not keep the tears from rolling down her cheeks. She felt betrayed and used again.

The doorbell rang and Avery went to the door wiping her tears with the back of her hands. When she opened the door,

Grant rushed in and grabbed her swinging her around and kissing her wildly. He didn't notice her tear streaked cheeks.

"I have never been so happy to see anyone in my life!" Grant was kissing Avery's neck and hugging her over and over again.

Avery giggled in delight and was thrilled to have her mood changed so quickly and wonderfully. "Grant, I am so happy you're home! I've missed you terribly! Come here, I have a surprise for you." Avery, smiling, led Grant into the kitchen. There on the kitchen island she had placed a sterling silver tray of fresh, home made chocolate chip cookies and a sterling silver tea pitcher on a silver trey containing fresh brewed Ahmad tea. She had placed two of her best china cups in their saucers on the trey along with two cloth napkins and silver teaspoons. In the center of the tea service lay a long stemmed single rose.

"Avery, you are an angel sent to me from above! Grant looked into Avery's face earnestly. This is so special. Thank you." Grant walked over to Avery who had moved to the opposite side of the island. He gently took her in his arms and held her sweetly. He stroked her hair as she nestled her head into the soft and warm crook of Grant's neck.

"Do you want to tell me why you have been crying?" Grant asked her softly.

Avery was surprised that Grant had noticed. "Oh, I was just angry with Meathead." She briefly told him what had just taken place over the phone.

"I understand, I have similar dealings with the female version of a meathead. Avery, you are a wonderful Mother and a very sweet person. I can see what is in your heart and I love what I see. We can deal with the meatheads if it means we will be together."

Grant could tell that Avery really didn't want to talk about it much so he gave her another hug, kissed her hair and led her to the bar stools where they fed each other chocolate chip cookies, laughed, talked and kissed. He wanted to show her how he felt about her so much more than kissing her, but the boys were upstairs in bed and he could not or would not take a chance of hurting Avery or the boys.

Around 10:30, Grant kissed Avery goodnight and left to go to his home that he had not seen for the last ten days. He was exhausted from his trip and the stress of the funeral. He had a huge day of catching up with patients tomorrow morning so after a warm shower, he went directly to bed. He would let his housekeeper unpack his bag and do the laundry tomorrow. He fell asleep almost immediately, but his last thoughts were of Avery.

He wanted to start getting the boys together with Avery and her sons. Blending the families would be fun. He would see if Avery and her boys could do something this weekend.

He also felt anger that Peter was so callous to Avery and he certainly understood her feelings; Tara was so much like Peter, they both seemed to blame someone else for their shortcomings, always wanting their way, and never able to accept the fact that they ever did anything wrong. It would be a challenge dealing with the ex husband and ex wife, but he felt certain they could deal with it. He was ready to take it on. He knew he had fallen in love with Avery. As he was drifting off to sleep he dreamed he saw Trent's face close to his saying. "It's going to be alright, Dad…" Comforting words from his son, and he knew that with Avery, it would be better than alright for all of them.

Grant called Avery on his lunch break around 12:30.

"Avery, how would you like to take the boys to dinner and to go bowling tomorrow night?"

"Are you kidding? They would love it!" Avery was delighted. "Mother and I were just discussing over the phone how to get the boys used to me dating. She felt the best way would be to include them in some of the things we do, so, what a great idea. You are so thoughtful!"

"I'm glad your mother would approve, I think she is a sage! Wonder if she knows how beautiful I think you are?"

"Do you really think I'm beautiful?" Avery asked, becoming coy.

"Have I never told you that I could pass a lot of time just looking at you?"

Avery laughed. "Grant, you are so sweet; did I tell you that I had a dream about my very handsome boyfriend last night?"

"What was the dream about?"

"Well, I had taken you in to see the tiles in my new bathroom and we started kissing wildly. We ended up rolling around naked in my bed and all of a sudden, you jumped up, put your clothes on and you said, "I can't do this!"

Grant looked surprised, "No! No, I didn't, I promise I didn't say that!"

Avery laughed hysterically. "So, you really were in my dream! You are much too cute!"

"Well, cute or not, I have to run, my nurse just came to drag me back to the examining room. I will dream of getting to see you naked all day! I'll e-mail you when I get a few seconds between patients today. Bye."

"Bye." Avery hung up the phone smiling. *He is sooooo wonderful!*

Bowling with all four boys was quite an experience. The party of six had to wait until a bowling lane came open before they could bowl, so they killed time eating hamburgers in the restaurant and trying to carry on some form of conversation between interruptions by the children.

Avery told Grant that Phil and Carrie, some friends of hers, had asked her out to dinner for tomorrow night and they had told her to invite Grant if he would like to come. They were actually anxious to meet him. Grant said that he would love to come to meet some of her friends. That was about the extent of any intelligent conversation between adults. The rest of the evening was spent playing and teasing the children.

Hunter and Trent, being the same age and with a love of sports in common, hit it off immediately and wrestled and rough housed all over the bowling alley. Avery and Grant gave Jason and Travis quarters and played video games with them for over an hour. When a bowling alley finally opened, Hunter and Trent showed off their nine year old, superior, athletic skills while Travis with his "nearly an adult at eleven" attitude scoffed at the immaturity of the younger boys.

Travis and Avery had some very interesting conversations about the kind of car Travis wanted when he was sixteen in between bowling turns.

Jason pouted, crossed his arms over his chest and would not bowl because there were no guards on the alley to lead his bowling ball to the pins. Avery wanted her sons to be angels tonight so she was a little more than embarrassed that Jason would not cooperate. She knew Jason was tired, and she was patient with him but she couldn't help but think, *this is the last time Grant will ever ask me and the boys to do anything with him again, and I don't blame him!* Avery tried to reason with Jason and coax him into just trying to bowl without the guards but he would have none of it! Just when Avery was starting to get exasperated, Grant walked over to Jason, picked him up and said, "Hey, fella, you don't have to bowl, but I sure would like it if you would help me."

"How do I help you, Mistow Gwant?"

"Well, you probably don't know this, but I am the boss of the Universe and if you help me, we can make that ball go just where we want it to go.

You sit here on my lap and help me figure out which way I need to throw my ball to make it knock all of those pins down. Can you do that?"

"I guess so, but oney if *you* thwo the ball!"

"Oh, I will, I promise, and I bet if you help me, we can beat those smarty pants nine year olds!"

"Yeah! Let's do it Mistow Gwant!"

Avery gave Grant a look of gratitude and her heart leaped for the man who would be so kind to her cranky and tired little darling.

From: Avery@aol.com
To: <gljclinic@aol.com>

Subject: great evening

Hello my handsome boyfriend, boss of the Universe.

We had so much fun last night. What a great family you have and I love how you remind them that you are the boss of the universe when you want them to do something. My kids really had a great time. Thank you so much for including us tonight. The burgers were great and the bowling was soooo much fun. I'm blowing you thank you kisses right now. It's three A.M.; guess you can tell I am not sleeping. I guess I am too wound up from all the fun tonight. I'm still hearing bowling balls crashing down the alley.

I can't wait to see you tonight.

I think you will enjoy having dinner with Phil and Carrie, so glad you wanted to come along. They are a wonderful couple and even though they are my friends through meathead in college days, they understand the situation and really want to meet you.

I know you won't want to be out too late since you have the boys this weekend, so maybe we can just eat and escape. We will have to budget our time wisely. I'm checking out and going back to bed.... I really need that beauty rest!

Love, Avery

From: "Grant Jones" <gljclinic@aol.com>

To: <Avery@aol.com>

Subject: Re: great evening

Hi back Princess.... we all had fun also. Travis and Trent both were eager to meet up with you guys. I can tell that Travis really wants to get to know you and likes you a lot. Thanks for spending time with him. I think he was showing off for you a little too, like you say that yours do. Trent loved playing with Hunter but I knew that he would of course, with Hunter around, he's not going to pay much attention to us (unless he wants quarters for the games) by the way, thank you for giving them all those quarters, that must have cost you a bundle!

I am looking forward to tonight. I am basically going to tell John, the sitter, that I will more than likely be out late. He will get the kids to bed for me.

Remember, Trent and Hunter play each other again tomorrow morning. Sooooo, I'll get to see you at the game too.

Can't wait till tonight...Love/Grant

Grant picked Avery up around 7:30 Saturday evening to go to dinner with her friends; Peter's friends. Grant was a little nervous, but had wanted to share everything with Avery, even if it meant he might be a little uncomfortable at times. His fears were unfounded. Phil and Carrie were very receptive of him and he enjoyed their company. They seemed to have a special marriage with mutual respect and were very proud of and into their children.

They had two sons, Hunter and Jason's ages and a set of twins who were three and into everything. One of the twins, and the only girl, Sophie, was the apple of Avery's eye. Avery loved to pick Sophie up while the boys were at school and take her shopping for things like feather boas and Cinderella crowns and slippers. Then, after a "girl" lunch, she would take Sophie home with her to paint fingernails and fix hair. Sophie adored Avery too and called her AAAAAver-i-ly. Sophie took the place of the little girl Avery had always wanted.

After dinner Avery and Grant came back to Avery's house and plopped on the couch in front of the fireplace. The boys had gone to spend the night with Peter since he couldn't have them next Wednesday night. The house was quiet and the only light was the flickering of the fire.

"Wow, Phil and Carrie have it going on, don't they?" Grant said to Avery as they sat down on her couch with a glass of Chablis.

"I knew you would like them, I got the feeling that they were impressed with you too."

"Do you think that Phil and Carrie just wanted to meet me so that they could report to Peter what our relationship is like?"

"No, not at all, Phil is a great friend of Peter's, they even went to high school together, but Phil is disappointed in what Peter has done and is doing. Phil and Carrie genuinely have my best interests at heart. I think they just wanted to make sure you were a nice person for their own peace of mind. We go to the same church, they are Catholic too. Maybe we can go together and meet them afterwards for lunch some Sunday."

"I would love that." Grant began nuzzling Avery's neck and kissing her softly.

"Grant, my girlfriends and I have planned a trip to Miami to watch the National Tennis finals next month. I have never been to Miami. I wish I were excited about going.....fun in the sun and all that."

"Really, you will love Miami. My sister's good friend from college lives in Miami. I have never been, but Katie says it is a fun place to be; tons of clubs and plenty to do, especially on South Beach."

"Sounds nice, but I think we will only be hitting the tennis matches. This sounds kind of crazy, but, oh, never mind."

"Tell me, you can't do this to me!"

"It's really just that I'm being silly. I am torn about going even though we planned it ages ago."

"How come?"

"I know I will miss you terribly. Is that too needy of me?"

"I think it's charming. Would you be able to stay a few more days if I could come to Miami to meet you after the tennis thing?"

Avery was shocked. She and Grant were getting closer, but they hadn't slept together yet; if she said for him to come, it would mean they would end up sleeping together whether they were ready or not. If she didn't let him come, she knew she would regret it. Avery knew in her heart that Grant was the kind of man she had dreamed of. She knew she could fall in love with him the first time she met him, if she would let herself, and after knowing him for only a couple of months, she knew she had fallen in love. She stammered "We..ll, I guess, if you want to."

"I want to."

Grant started kissing Avery on her neck, he worked up to her lips and deeply and passionately kissed her over and over again. Avery felt herself reel with desire and passion. They felt for each other and found a mutual place where all the hurt and loneliness dissolved into their kisses of desire.

"Avery, I love you," Grant whispered in her ear.

"I am so happy to hear you say that, but you know, it doesn't really mean anything in the heat of passion."

"I know", Grant whispered between kisses, but you'll see, I love you with my whole being, Avery."

Avery felt herself falling deeper and deeper into oblivion. They kissed and caressed until neither of them could stand it any longer.

"Avery, I want to love you forever." the words from Grant's hot breath in between his warm, soft kisses and passionate need opened Avery's heart to take him in her arms and hold him. She wanted to crawl inside of him; to feel him inside of her.

She led him by the hand to her bedroom. They stood embracing next to the bed where he kissed her on her neck and her lips and her chest, and his breath was sweet and warm and heavy. She undressed him slowly and carefully and he let her before he started undressing her. He kissed her softly and gently as they laid on the bed. He rubbed the soft skin on her sides and felt the curve of her tiny waist. She rubbed his back with both of her hands and ran her fingernails from his waist to his shoulders as she pulled him closer to her. "Avery", Grant moaned with desire as he rolled gently on top of her. Avery's breath was short and uneven. They sank deeper into her feather soft bed where they made love over and over and over again and he held her through the night like a child clinging to her for his life. She felt a security and a love that she had not known before and he felt a deep fulfillment and a deep love that he knew Avery shared.

"Ohhhh," Grant moaned. "Avery, sweetheart, it' 3 AM and I have to go let John go home!" Grant was pulling on his pants.

"Huh? Oh, I hope he doesn't hate us for staying out so late" A sleepy Avery answered.

"Yea, me too, he is a great baby-sitter, I'd hate to lose him."

Avery pulled a sheet around her and got up to walk Grant to the door. She felt a little awkward being naked in front of him, even though they had just made love. At the door Grant stopped to kiss her warmly on the lips but he stopped to earnestly look in her eyes before he said, "Avery, I love you, does that count for anything now?"

"That counts for everything now. I love you too, Grant. I think you knew that didn't you?" she asked smiling up at him.

"I only hoped. Goodnight my love. He kissed her once more. "Thank you for loving me."

Avery locked the door behind him, looked up to heaven and said to God "Thank you for sending that man to me; please let him be real and please don't let him change."

CHAPTER 7

Monday morning Avery slipped into a pair of deep color blue jeans and a soft peach cashmere sweater. She hurriedly scooted her feet into a pair of leather slides and swooped her shoulder length hair back into a casual ponytail at the back of her neck. Then a little dab of coral lipstick and a touch of eye make-up, and she was ready for the day.

Avery was that lucky sister the family called the golden girl. Not only because life seemed to always be good to her, at least before Peter's affair, but because her skin had that golden glow; like she had a hint of a tan all year long. Her skin was silky smooth and the peach of the cashmere sweater brought out the gold in her brown eyes and made the skin over her cheeks take on the look of a dusty pink rose petal. Her smoothed back hair was blonde, really a honey color, with light blonde highlights that shimmered in the light. Avery was a golden girl and all who met her knew it.

After Avery dropped the kids off at school she met her friends Lisa and Janie for coffee at the Bagel Hut. They were always eager to hear the latest on the "love birds".

Janie and Lisa were already sipping on a cup of hot cappuccino when Avery entered the small café'. The girls were seated in a booth at the far corner away from the order bar for privacy. The Bagel hut had been a small boutique before so the owners had little decorating to do to get the stylish effect they wanted for their café.

"Hey girls! Gosh, Lisa, I'm glad you could make it today, I was afraid you would have to go show a house or go to a closing or something."

"Not this early, but I can't stay long." Lisa answered.

Janie and Lisa were a mixed matched pair. Petite Janie, wore a pair of faded blue jeans with a royal blue, long sleeve T-shirt speckled with rhinestones spelling "Queen Mother". Her short blonde hair was tossed in an expensive Meg Ryan "I never comb my hair" look, and her thin lips were perfectly lined with pale pink lipstick inside the lines. The combination of pinks and blues made her big blue eyes seem even larger as they glimmered in anticipation of what she would learn from Avery today.

Lisa, the eternal real estate agent, had no children and worked as a diversion to boredom. She was a beautiful girl of French and Italian decent, as most Baton Rouge natives were, with a lovely olive complexion, chic, jaw length brown hair and hazel eyes with long lashes and well-defined eyebrows. Her lips were naturally full, accented with a barely red lipstick and very little makeup. Lisa was rarely seen wearing anything but a tailored business suit. Today she had chosen a navy blue Jones of New York, navy high heel shoes and a pale pink silk blouse, which made her slightly plump body look slimmer and gave her the professional look of the successful Realtor that she was.

"OK, girl, how were your dates this weekend?" Janie asked with a little glint in her eyes as she leaned into the table toward Avery.

"Absolutely fabulous! I can't believe it, but I think he stepped right out of the pages of a romance novel. I am so in love!" Avery gladly gave the girls that information.

"I think it's time you made him a home cooked dinner,"

"I'm ahead of you there, Lisa, I've already cooked two of them for him and he at least *acted* like he liked them. To be honest, one meal turned out great and the other just so so."

"Well?" Janie wanted more scoop.

"Well, what?" Avery teased.

"You know darn well *what!*" Janie was leaning in further with a grin. "Did you sleep with him?"

"Janie, you know I'm not going to tell you that!" Avery was turning a little red from embarrassment.

"Well, for God sakes, Janie, she shouldn't give herself to him on a silver platter!" retorted Lisa. "She has only known him for two months, if that!"

"What's two months if she is crazy about him?" Janie turned to Lisa to argue her point.

"I've just heard that he is quite a ladies man, that's all. I just want Avery to be extremely careful."

"Well, if I recall, Lisa, you were the one who said he was such a good catch!" snapped Janie.

"Helloooo, I'm sitting right here, girls. Lisa, what have you heard?' Avery showed a little concern in her voice.

"Oh, nothing much, just that he has dated a lot of women. I just don't want you to get hurt."

"I appreciate your concern. I don't want to get hurt either. Lisa, are you sure you are telling me everything you know?"

"I've just heard that he has had several one night stands, and then a few hot and heavy flings and that a couple of girls even thought he was going to marry him. I just don't want you to be another notch in his stethoscope, that's all."

Avery began feeling that old insecurity in her gut. Her thoughts were swirling. *My God, I just gave my heart, soul and body to him. I thought I could tell what was in his heart. Wouldn't I be able to tell if he wasn't sincere? Shit, I was the last to know that Peter was lying and cheating on me. Maybe my judgment is not as good as I thought. How stupid can I be! What in the hell was I thinking! Shit, shit, shit!* She began to get a sick feeling in the pit of her stomach. It seemed to Avery that she had been so up and down lately. One minute full of doubt and the next minute totally sure of what she was doing.

Lisa checked her watch. "Opps; I do have to go now, y'all call me later. Bye girls."

Avery managed a weak smile as Lisa jumped up from the table and rushed for to make her appointment.

Janie yelled to Lisa before she made it to the door, "Hey, do you want to come by after work and play some gin rummy with me?"

No, I can't, Bob is coming home early tonight and I have to cook supper. That man would starve to death before he would make himself a sandwich!" Lisa smiled and waved goodbye while rushing out of the door.

"Hey, Ave, don't mind her, she really doesn't know him, you know." Janie could sense the inner turmoil Avery was feeling.

"Janie, I did sleep with him. He seems so totally honest and sincere. Could I be so wrong about his intentions?"

"Look, Avery, we all make mistakes. If you made a mistake you will know soon enough, if he is sincere, you will know that too. I think you are a great judge of character. Look at the messes you have gotten me out of with some not so sincere guys!" Janie had been divorced twice and was having a hard time meeting anyone serious.

"I just hope you're right, Janie. I don't think I could stand it if I was letting myself be used."

"I think you have been extremely careful. Quit worrying about that! How do you, or should I say how *did* you feel about sleeping with him?"

"Really?"

"Uh…., yeah!"

"Well, it was wonderful! He was so tender and so unselfish. He didn't just get what he wanted and roll over like Peter did. He was so sweet. He told me he loved me for the first time last night, and I really think he meant it. And afterward, he held me so closely I could hardly breathe. He made me feel so secure. It was heaven."

"Wow, sounds wonderful."

"It was. I just hope to God that I haven't rushed into this on hope instead of facts. He does seem too good to be true, and that does scare me. But, Janie, you know, I have too much responsibility to get married right away. I should probably be feeling guilty for having sex, but I am having to re-think my morality issues. I can't rush into a marriage. I have to think of the boys."

"I know, I know, how did you feel this morning? Did you have that *what in the hell have I done* feeling?"

"No, not at all. I felt so much calmer and more at ease than I have felt in ages."

"Must be love, then." Janie smiled in approval of Avery.

"Would you think I was totally stupid if I told you that I would not have slept with him if I didn't really think that I am in love with him?"

That evening after the boys were tucked into bed Avery went to the computer to check her e-mail. She had been running all day and this was the first chance she had to sit and relax. Grant had called a couple of times on her cell during the day between patients. He was so very attentive to her. She had decided to take things as they came and not to worry about what Lisa had said. She would ask him, however, when the time was right about how many other women there had been; for Avery, their relationship could not move on without complete trust and honesty.

From: "Grant L Jones"gljonesclinic@aol.com>
To:<Avery@aol.com

Sent: Monday January 26, 6:30 AM

Subject: Hi

I woke up this morning and felt for you beside me. You weren't there. What a bummer. Have I told you lately what a wonderful dream come true you gave to me. Have I told you lately that I love you? Well, I do. I am hopelessly at your mercy.

I have been going through your e-mails to me and I didn't get a chance to reply to the one while I was in Georgia. I did feel compelled to discuss the tennis pro thing with Katie, and while she did have a lot of fun with that, you will be glad to know that she didn't fall off her bar stool and break her hip from laughing so hard.

You mentioned needs, and I understand that. Needs are powerful and will make you do things you might not do ordinarily. I also know that there are a lot of guys out there who would zero in on an opportunity to take advantage of an emotionally starved woman, especially one as attractive as you are. You were probably right to throw the water on that flame. I'm so glad you did. Hopefully, we are not judged by our mistakes, but by what is in our hearts. I think there is only beauty in your heart, Avery. By the way, I have made some mistakes too, and have some regrets, but I really try to keep on the straight and narrow. About having fun, my worldly eleven year old who saw his little cousin put a plastic bag over his head said "don't do that, you could smother and die with a plastic bag over your head and then, you couldn't play and have fun!"

I guess the analogy of me telling you this is that being in a bad marriage, or relationship, is like having a plastic bag over your head, do you agree?

Anyway, live and learn. I agree with you that relationships based on need won't work. It has to be based on mutual respect, complete trust and love. And of course, there needs to be fun. I just want you to know that with you, I think that I have all of the above. You have taken the plastic bag off of my head and I thank you so very much! I'll call you tonight when I think you have the kids to bed.

I love you, GLJ

Gosh, it's like he reads my mind! He is so intuitive! The phone interrupted Avery's thoughts. She looked at the clock; it was almost 9:00PM. *Must be Grant*, she thought.

"Hello."

"Avery, th-this is Lisa. Could you co-ome over here? They have just taken Bob to the hospital and, and Avery, he's d-dead!" Lisa was sobbing at the other end of the phone line.

"I'll be right there." Avery felt her hair standing on ends, her blood raced through her veins to the top of her head.

She hung up the phone and grabbed the boys out of bed. "Bring your pillows with you guys and you can sleep in the car." She half dragged and half carried the sleeping boys from their beds to the car for the short trip to Lisa's house. In the car she called Peter.

"Peter, could you please come by Lisa's and get the boys to spend the night with you?' Lisa just called and she said Bob is dead, I am on my way to her house now."

"Avery, it's too late to be getting the boys out. Just stay home with them, you don't need to go over there!"

"Never mind, Peter." Avery hung up the phone and called her sitter Christine. "Christine, I know it's late, but do you think you could come over to my friend Lisa's to pick up the boys and take them back home to bed? Do you remember where she lives?"

"Yes, I remember. Why, what's the matter?"

"Lisa's husband has just died."

"My God, I'll be over there in about thirty minutes."

"Could you spend the night, I don't know how long I will be?"

"Sure, Avery, I'll be there in 10 minutes."

"Thank you so much Chris, I wouldn't ask you, but Peter wouldn't come to get them."

"That ass hole! What a jerk! I'll be there right away."

Christine adored Avery. Christine worked at the tennis club where Avery played and when they met they became fast friends. Christine coached the boys in tennis and she worked inside scheduling appointment for the tennis pros. Christine was nearly twenty and had done nothing else since she graduated from high school except work at the club and baby-sit.

She was slightly attractive but plump with short brown hair and small eyes. She was a little bit of a tomboy. She had few dates and Avery felt very lucky that most of the time when she needed a sitter, Chris was available. She had fixed Chris up several times on blind dates, but somehow, they never stuck around.

Avery parked the car in Lisa's carport and left the sleeping boys in the car. She cracked the windows a little and locked the car doors. Then, she rushed into Lisa's house where she found a hysterical Lisa and a couple of neighbors all in their robes.

"Lisa, do we need to get to the hospital?" Avery asked her friend.

"N-no-no, th-they told me he was dead. I- I'm suppose to wait and go t-to the funeral ho-home in a couple of hours." Lisa's speech was hardly audible between sobs.

"Lisa, I'm so sorry. What happened, can you tell me yet?"

Lisa sniffed and tried to compose herself. Avery waited while Lisa dabbed at her tears and went to the door to check on the boys. As Avery walked back to Lisa she began telling what had happened.

"We h-had just had a won-wonderful dinner and we w-were sitting in front of the TV holding hands. Bob said he was really ti-tired and wa-wanted to go to bed to watch the rest of the TV program. I said that was fine with me, I wanted to read anyway, so we w-went to bed. After the show was over, Bob asked me to rub his back; he said he f-felt like he had a little indigestion so I rubbed his ba-back and he rolled over and I thought he started snoring right away. I rubbed his hand a little and he quit snoring and made this funny sound. I didn't th-think anything of it and started reading my book. After a while, I reached for his ha-hand again and, *Avery,* it was so cold! Lisa continued to sob.

Avery pushed the hair away from Lisa's wet cheeks and asked, "What did you do then?"

"I covered him up and kissed his temple and then, I didn't hear him breathing. Avery, he was *d-dead!*" Lisa's body convulsed in sorrowful sobs; she wailed and cried until no tears were left. Avery sat next to her on the couch and held her like a child. She stroked her hair and rocked her and they cried together.

Avery caught a glimpse of Christine's headlights out of the window and left for a few minutes to help Christine with the boys.

"Lisa, I'm back." Avery went back to sit by Lisa on the couch and started rubbing her back as Lisa sobbed into her hands.

"Lisa, have you told Bob's mother yet?"

"Avery, you know Bob's mother is dying in the hospital of cancer. We just put her in the hospital yesterday and I just can't bring myself to tell her yet!"

"It's OK, Lisa, just do what you have to do right now. Let me know when you need to go tell her and I will go with you."

"Thank you, Avery, maybe tomorrow."

Bob was about ten years older than Lisa. They had married later in life and had no children. Lisa had been busy with her real estate career and Bob was and investment banker. He was in great shape, a runner. No one ever suspected he had a heart defect. Lisa and Bob had what most people dream of in a marriage. The two were perfectly compatible and enjoyed being together. Bob loved Lisa just the way she was, fun and lively and Lisa loved Bob for his intelligence and his good nature. Lisa would be lost without Bob.

Avery went to the funeral home with Lisa to choose a casket and to make the other arrangements. The two girls came back to Lisa's where they called her mother and sisters to break the bad news. One of Lisa's sisters lived a short distance away in Hammond and would be there in a couple of hours and her mother and other sister would be there in the morning. Avery called Grant to fill him in and then stayed until Lisa's sister came in around 1:00 A.M. After meeting Lisa's sister, Avery left and went straight to Grant's.

"Hi, Baby, you OK?" Grant met her at the door. "How is Lisa doing?" He led her to the kitchen where he poured them both a glass of wine. Then they walked to his couch in front of the fireplace and talked as the flames from the gas logs flickered and made shadows dance on the walls of the cozy gathering room. "Well, she is doing as well as expected, I guess. She is kind of numb right now. Did I tell you that Lisa and Bob just put his mother in the hospital day before yesterday? She is dying with cancer. I told Lisa I would go with her tomorrow when she tells her mother-in-law that Bob has died. She is dreading that so much. It will probably kill his mother."

"Man, when it rains it pours sometimes."

"Oh, Grant, I feel so sorry for Lisa, what will she do without Bob?"

"I don't know. Do you think she will be alright financially?"

"Yes, financially she will be fine, that's not what I'm worried about. They had such a good marriage. She will never find that again. They had what I want and now he is gone. It's gone." Tears began streaming down Avery's cheeks for her friend.

Grant put his arms around her and held her. She knew what it was like to be alone. She knew how hard it was to find someone who really cared about you and someone you could really care about. How hard it was to find someone who could really love you for where you came from and for what you are like on the inside, for who you are.

Avery looked up at Grant "I guess that is why I wanted to come by tonight. I want to let you know that I have been doing a lot of thinking lately. Especially after the other night, everyone keeps telling me that I need to be so careful because I'm surely not healthy after being divorced for such a short time. Grant, is there something that is suppose to hit me now? Am I being unrealistic in thinking that we have something special?"

"I don't think you are being unrealistic at all. I feel the same way, Avery"

"Grant, I know that we have only been seeing each other for a couple of months, but since Bob died, I want to tell you this."

"What, baby?" Grant pushed a piece of her hair from her cheek as she talked.

"Grant, I do get really scared sometimes because I don't know how I am supposed to know if I am really in love except by the way I feel. All I know is that you are the kindest, gentlest and sweetest man I have ever known. I love being with you. You make me comfortable, even making love the other night; instead of me feeling guilty, you made me feel beautiful. If you were to happen to die tonight, I want you to know that I have thanked God for sending you to me. And I want to thank you for coming into my life."

Avery began rambling "Sorry, I know I got a little deep, but I had to say those things, now, you can dump me, throw me out..............."

"Avery, I'm not going anywhere. I'm here, and I'm here for you. Thank you for trusting me. I feel that you were sent to me too."

Grant kissed Avery's tear stained cheeks, and she kissed his full, warm lips and all of their emotions exploded as they made love on his couch.

"Hey, you can make house calls over here anytime you want to." Grant grinned at Avery as she walked out of the door to go home.

"Thanks, Doctor Jones! It's a miracle! I'm cured!" Avery teased as she walked to her car.

As Grant closed the back door he thought he heard his youngest son call to him. "Dad, Dad." It was a soft, young almost girlish voice. Grant looked upstairs on the way to his room and realized the boys were with their mother tonight. *Jesus, I'm hearing things!* He thought as he shook his head and went on to his room for the night.

The ride home seemed very long tonight. Avery was emotionally and physically exhausted. Her thoughts were of Lisa and how very sad and lonely her life would be now without Bob and without any children. Avery said "thank you prayers" that she had her children and Grant, at least for now, and when her tired mind wouldn't let her think anymore, the words from the psalm ran through her head over and over again. *Even though I walk through the valley of the shadow of death, I will fear no evil......*

CHAPTER 8

Early the next morning Avery took the children to school and stopped by Lisa's house. She was relieved to see that Lisa's family had all made it in and that Lisa was much better now, surrounded by her mother, sisters, and her supportive family. Avery knew that Lisa would need her much more after the funeral when everyone had gone back home.

Lisa introduced Avery to everyone and after a short visit, Avery left to go home and take care of some personal business. She needed to clean the house that she had left in an uproar since last night.

"Thank you so much for coming and for being here for me last night, Avery. My sisters said they would go with me to the hospital to tell Bob's mother so you're off the hook today, Ok?."

"That's fine, Lisa, just call me if you need me.

"You know I will."

Avery walked in the door to her quiet house and immediately the phone started ringing. Avery had thought many times that without a phone her life would be so much easier. The phone for Avery, much of the time, was a frustration rather than a convenience mainly because it rang incessantly.

"Hello."

"Hey Avery, it's Mom. How are things?"

"Mom, do you remember my friend, Lisa? She is my real estate agent who helped us to find this house?"

"Sure I do."

"Her husband, Bob, died last night and I was up till all hours with her. I came home this morning to clean up a little and I think I'll take a nap after while too."

"I'm so sorry to hear that. Wasn't he pretty young?"

"Yes, it was totally unexpected. He had a heart defect that no one knew about. Mom, it's so sad. They had just had a great dinner together, she said they held hands while they watched TV and he wanted to go to bed early. He died right after they went to bed."

"Oh, Avery, how terrible! Was he overweight?"

"No, that's just it, he was in great shape. He was a runner and took really good care of himself."

"Please tell Lisa how very sorry I am, and tell her this; your grandfather used to say that sometimes, God picks the most beautiful roses for his garden first. For some reason that thought gave me comfort when your little sister died. Maybe it will make Lisa feel a little better too."

"Thanks, Mom, I'll tell her that."

"Well, you sound terribly tired. Real quickly, how is Grant?"

"Mother, he is totally wonderful. I had a sitter for the boys last night so I went by his house after I left Lisa. He is the sweetest man I have ever met. He is the most understanding man, so kind, and sympathetic. I really adore him"

"That is great. Hey, the reason I called was to tell you that I sent you an e-mail of your love horoscope. You need to read it when you have time. It's really hilarious, and kind of risqué for you mother to be reading!"

"Oh, really? Then, I'll go pull it up right now!"

"Just do it when you have a minute to laugh. Go get some rest, and give the boys a kiss for me. OK?"

"Speaking of the boys, I'm thinking of bringing them home this weekend. I have to go to a child psychologist with Peter Friday, he seems to think that I am ruining the kid's lives lately. Grant has his sons this weekend so after I pick the boys up from school, I think I will just head on to St. Charles, if that's OK with you."

"You know that will be great with me, your dad will love to see you, but what about Bob's funeral? Won't you be going to that?"

"No, they are having his funeral in Texas where he was raised. Then he will be buried in the family plot. At least that is the plan right now."

"Well, let me know about the funeral arrangements, OK?"

"Sure. Well, I guess I'll see you this weekend. I'll be in around 7:00 Friday night. Thanks for calling. Love you."

"Love you too, bye."

Jimmie knew her daughter. She sounded stressed and exhausted. Hopefully, Avery would take a nap and not get sidetracked into doing something else.

Jimmie would make sure that she would get plenty of rest this weekend at home. She would have Liza and Piper take the boys to play with their kids, so the boys would have and their mother could get some rest.

To: Avery@aol.com

From: Jimreal@valco.net

Forward: Love horoscope

LOVE MATCHES OF THE STARS

Here it is: the basic compatibility of the two star signs you have chosen. Of course this description is fairly general, but it should help you avoid a bad pairing or take advantage of a good one.

SCORPIO (Oct 24- Nov22) and TAURUS (Apr 21- May 21)

This pairing can put hairs on the chest of almost anyone. These two signs attract each other from opposite ends of the zodiac, and you know what they say about opposites! Well, these two can attract each other like maddened magnets, and you only have to look at their rulers to know why. Taurus is ruled by Venus, who answers to amour and fatal attractions, while Scorpio, on the other hand, is ruled by the powerful, psychological, and single-minded, sexy Mars. Imagine the rulers of love and sex tripping through tulips, fantastic together and you will begin to see what a winner this one can be.

Because these are both fixed folk, their relationship will be fantastically faithful and gorgeously generous. It'll also be primarily possessive, though that might not cause as many setbacks as you would think. Both signs want to possess the other, not only physically, but also on a more mental level.

The wonderful thing is that they both love it! I hear all of those airy amours saying "How primitive!" The problem comes (yes, dear, there usually is one-after all, when they said the path of true love never did run smooth they weren't talking about lumpy lawns!) If the Plutonian is a bit of a playboy or playgirl, the minute the truth comes out world war 3 will erupt! There is rigidity to this relationship; it's intrinsically intransigent and ferociously fixed. These two believe that they've been welded together for life and it will take more than a hammer and a chisel to prize them apart.

The key to this couple's connubial bliss is for them both to adopt outside interests and not to be dependent on each other for both leisure and pleasure. Because they both strive for security (home is where the heart is for blissful Bulls), they'll want to be together a lot, but they must give their relationship a chance to breathe by broadening their horizons.

(Just as long as temptation isn't lurking around the corner in the guise of another amour both of them find it hard to be attracted to someone seemingly insincere,

However, either of them cannot detach the body beautiful from the bubbly brain. Either way, though, this is a prosaically poochy pairing with unkempt earthy desire. Put a Bull boy with a Scorpio girl and you'll get something so sexy and steamy that it will knock your socks off. This is a combination to corrupt Geronimo.

Lisa called Avery shortly after 2:00 o'clock. Avery had actually been taking a nap before she had to pick up the boys at school today. Fortunately, Jason was staying in "after care" a couple of days a week for his speech therapy.

"Hey Avery, I just had to call you. You won't believe what has happened."

"What?" Avery was rubbing her sleepy eyes.

"Well, we went to Bob's mother's room at the hospital and she was feeling well enough to sit up in bed. I said to her "Mamma, *I came to tell you something about Bob.*"

Ave, she said, *"Honey, you don't have to tell me. I know Bob is in heaven. I saw him in my room last night. He is fine and you are going to be fine too."*

I couldn't do anything but to hug her and cry. She didn't shed a tear. She just comforted me!"

"Oh, Lisa, how beautiful. How lucky you are to know that." Avery was amazed at what she had just heard but she didn't doubt it in the least.

"We are leaving in the morning for Texas for Bob's funeral and buria.l" Lisa started to cry. "Oh, Avery, what am I going to do without Bob?"

Lisa, you must think of Bob now, remember what his mother told you, ok?"

."Ok, I'll try. It's just so hard and I'm so scared. Anyway Ave, I'll call you when I get home."

"Lisa, I am so sorry, are you going to be OK?"

"You know, once I talked to Mamma at the hospital, it was kind of like comforting. I will miss Bob terribly, but I have some an inner peace now."

"I'm glad, Lisa. Bob was a wonderful guy and my mother said to tell you that God picks only the most beautiful flowers for his garden, I think Bob was a beautiful flower."

"Oh, Avery, he was! What a beautiful way to express it! Please thank your mother for me."

'I will."

"Ok, I better go. I'll call you next week."

"Bye, Lisa. My prayers are with you."

That night, over the phone Avery told Grant the story Lisa had told her about Bob's mother and asked Grant if he had ever come across anything like that in the hospitals with any of his patients. He told her he had not, but that he would like to believe that things like that happened.

"I have the afternoon off tomorrow, why don't you come over to my house for lunch and spend the afternoon with me?" Grant was anxious to have Avery to himself, even if it was for a couple of hours.

"Sounds like fun, I'll bring lunch, a big old greasy cheeseburger with fries and malt. OK?"

"Yea, anything you want." Grant grimaced at the thought of the grease. Just then, he had a flashback of one of the nurses at the hospital looking directly into his face saying, "Dr. Jones, it is almost lunch time.." Avery's voice shook him back to reality.

"Oh, no, you don't, I see you daydreaming of a big fat burger and fries. It will be more like a salad topped with chicken; someone has to take care of *your* heart!" Avery laughed.

"Hey, Princess, Tara is trading me nights with the boys so she can go to a party, tomorrow night, so I won't have the boys until Thursday night and through the weekend, would you consider staying here with me tomorrow night after you take the boys to Peter?"

"I would love to but what would your neighbors think. I know the girl next door."

Grant laughed, "I doubt they would think a thing since they shacked up over there a while before they got married."

"Grant, you are a devil! Could I park my car in your garage?"

"Of course you can, you wild and crazy woman!" Grant found Avery's concern over the neighbors seeing her car at his house amusing. He couldn't quit smiling. "OK, I'll come around 6:00. I should have the boys to Peter by then."

Grant was a practical man in most respects. He was very intelligent, but not outwardly what you would call an intellectual. He had seen some death because of the nature of his profession. Being a cardiologist in a large city meant that some of his patients would not live long, but most of the time they were older and death wasn't so unexpected. He felt for Lisa and her loss. He regretted that he had never met Bob.

The Baton Rouge General hospital on Blue Bonnet and his office were both close to the Baton Rouge Country Club and to Grant's home. He loved the convenience of their locations. There was only one problem, Tara lived only a few blocks away from his home and he knew she kept up with what was going on at his house because he would catch her driving by on more than one occasion. When he purchased his home, he thought it would be a great idea to be close to his children, but now, he regretted his decision in some ways.

Grant got home Wednesday around 11:30 and was glad he would have time to take a shower and change from the hospital scrubs to a pair of comfortable sweat pants and t-shirt before Avery arrived with lunch.

He couldn't believe how nervous and excited he was to get to spend an afternoon with her. Grant was putting shaving lotion on his face in his sumptuous bathroom when he heard Avery knocking on his back door.

"Hellewwww," Avery called as she opened the back door and walked in.

Grant dabbed his face with the cream-colored hand towel that Maria, his housekeeper so carefully laid out for looks and he tossed it on the counter before rushing to meet Avery in the kitchen.

"Hi, love!" Grant came up behind Avery and put his arms around her waist and started kissing her neck while she opened the sack of turkey sandwiches at the kitchen counter.

"I bet you are starving!" Avery turned, smiling, to plant some kisses of her own.

"Only for you." Grant and Avery embraced and kissed all the way to the bedroom."

"I've got to go pick up the kids, it almost 3:00!" exclaimed Avery as she stretched her legs and pulled herself away from Grants hold on her in the bed. She laughed as she played tug of war with Grant for the sheet to cover her before getting out of bed. He finally let her win and she wrapped herself in the sheet, and started picking her clothes up off the floor where they lay scattered from the door way. She quickly dressed in his bathroom and went back to the bedroom to find Grant dressed and ready to walk her to the door. "Thanks for the wonderful lunch." Grant smiled as he told her. I can't wait till you get back."

"I won't be long, I promise."

A quick kiss and she was gone. It was a wonderful feeling having a woman around his house. Not just any woman, Avery Lyons. Peter ate one of the turkey sandwiches still sitting on the kitchen counter and started thinking about plans for the night. His cell phone rang and he answered, thinking it was the hospital. "Hello, this is Dr. Jones."

"Grant, I've decided to send Travis away to camp for a month this summer in Georgia. It's a great camp where they not only learn to ride horses and camp out and swim and boat. It's a camp where they learn technical things like some computer programming, how to build a web site, and some business skills. I need you to pay half. The total cost is around $4,000. If you pay me $2,500, I will take him and pick him up."

"Tara, I really think that he is a little young to be gone from us for a month! What does he say about it?"

"He wants to go, naturally!"

"Why a camp so far from home?"

"Grant, Good grief! If you don't care anymore about your son than to not let him go to the best camp there is, then just forget about it! You only care how much money it is going to cost you!"

"Tara, the money is not the issue here. I just think he is too young to be going so far away."

"That's your problem, you treat him like a small child. He is almost twelve years old! Don't think that he doesn't notice that he and Trent have had to take a back seat since you have been dating Avery. You tell him that you won't pay for him to go to camp because you are spending all of your money on Avery and **her** kids!"

"Tara, I will pay for him to go to camp, if he really wants to go. I just hope he doesn't get too homesick."

"He is not a baby anymore, Grant. Thank you. I'll tell him that he gets to go."

"OK, Tara, bye."

"Good buy."

Avery picked the boys up from school and they came home to work on their homework while she fixed their favorite meal; chicken strips, green beans and macaroni and cheese. She took a quick shower, stuffed a toothbrush, a fresh pair of underwear, and a cute little teddy pajama in an overnight bag. *What am I doing?* She thought. *The boys will wonder where I am going to spend the night!* She dumped out the contents of the overnight bag and stuffed them into her purse. She then packed the boy's bags for the night at their dad's. She called Peter on his cell phone and found out he would be a little late so she and the boys stopped by a boutique where she bought a few things for Grant's bedroom. His home was beautiful, but his bedroom was sparsely decorated. She found a handsome leather chest, a beautiful; leather bound antique book, and small pot of ivy that would all look splendid on his new, vacant nightstand.

Avery was a little nervous about spending all night at Grant's house. She was raised to be modest and felt a little awkward making herself at home in someone else's domain. She was, however looking forward to spending time with Grant alone and couldn't wait to give him the gifts for his bedside table. Apprehension filled her chest as she turned her car into his short driveway. She couldn't help but worry about the neighbors seeing her car there. The homes in his neighborhood were all large, elegant homes. Some were new, like Grant's, but most of them were older estate homes built on small lots. *I'm so glad that Grant bought the house next to him and tore it down so that he could have a nice yard. Too bad his driveway isn't on that side of the house where there are no neighbors!* Avery's mind was whirling as she pulled up to the garage door and stopped. Just at that moment, the garage door started its slow assent up into the ceiling of the garage. *Oh, thank God, I can pull into the garage. That sweet Grant, he was waiting to open the door for me, knowing that I am nervous about this. He is so thoughtful!*

Grant was standing in the doorway of the garage and kitchen when Avery jumped down from the tall seats of the

Expedition. "Grant, thank you so much for that, you are so sweet!"

"I am so lucky, you mean." Grant leaned against the wall by the opener smiling at Avery.

"And, how is that?" Avery grinned with a cocky wiggle.

"That you came!" Grant smiled as she walked past him into the house.

"I have a prize for you, Grant."

"I love surprises! What is it?" Grant asked, excitedly.

"Come here and I will show you." Avery led Grant into his massive bedroom. "Now close your eyes and I will tell you when to look."

Grant did as she asked and she unloaded the sacks she had carried in under her arms. She took the leather box and ivy and book and arranged them on the empty bedside table. "You can look now."

Grant opened his eyes and was thrilled that Avery had gone to the trouble to shop for him. Not only did he love the surprise, but also he liked the taste she displayed in the items she had purchased for him. It had been so very long since anyone had done anything nice for him like that.

"Thank you so much, my princess. I should be buying you gifts instead of you doing it for me." Avery could tell he was very pleased and it made her terribly happy.

Grant and Avery walked to the little restaurant on the corner of his neighborhood where they shared another wonderful meal and several glasses of good wine. On the way home, they held hands and walked slowly, enjoying the early signs of spring. They laughed at the children playing in the back yards and nodded to the neighbors who power walked past them with bandannas around their heads. They stopped at the corner movie rental store and rented a movie. Once they got back to Grant's house they watched a movie lounging together on the couch. They kissed and played and talked about their boys. Avery brought a copy of the love horoscope that her mother had sent her. They read it and laughed together. Then they got on the computer and looked up a compatibility love test that they agreed they passed with flying colors. Grant invited Avery to a cocktail party at the New Orleans Repertoire Theater for the next week and they decided to go to bed around 10:00.

Avery went into the bath first to change into the teddy she brought and brush her teeth. As she closed the door to the bathroom, she noticed a small, pink terry cloth bathrobe hanging on the door with the size tags still attached and a note. *Hope this fits better than the sheet. I love you, Grant.* "Grant!" Avery screamed from the bathroom. "Thank you so much! I love it!" She came bounding out of the bathroom wearing her new short, fluffy robe and bounced on the bed by Grant nearly knocking him off. "You angel! You are the sweetest man in the whole world!"

Grant laughed and took Avery in his arms. "You had to have something to lounge around in tomorrow morning while I'm at work. I want you to sleep late and stay here in the morning until you have to pick up Jason."

"Ooooh, so I get to be lazy in the morning, huh? It won't be as much fun if you can't be lazy with me." Avery faked a big pout."

"Just practice for when I can, OK?"

When Avery woke in the morning she felt for Grant in the empty spot where he had slept next to her. She rolled over and noticed it was almost 7:30 AM.

She got up smiling while she put on her new robe and went to the kitchen where she found some gourmet coffees Grant had set out on the kitchen counter for her. *Yep, he walked right out of a romance novel. I'm going to have to pinch myself. I hope he doesn't change.*

Avery had found herself smiling much more these days than in the past few years and months. It was great to have so much to smile about these days! She went to the door to see if the newspaper had been thrown on the front porch. The paper was there but it was several feet away from the porch, on the sidewalk, about half way between the porch and the street. She hurriedly walked down the steps and the sidewalk to pick it up. Just as she was standing up with the paper in her hand, she noticed a car driving by very slowly. She got a glimpse of the driver and passengers just before the car sped off towards the corner. *Damn, Damn, Damn! Grant will have hell to pay, now!* Avery was sick at her stomach. Tara, Travis and Trent were all staring at her with their mouths wide open just before they sped off.

Avery immediately called Grant to warn him of impending trouble.

"Don't worry about it Avery, I don't owe her a thing. She was probably going to drop the kids off for me to take to school for her. Maybe that will teach her to quit taking for granted that I am here to be her personal slave."

Friday morning promptly at 8:30 A.M. Peter met Avery at Dr. Jane Sizemore's office.

"Hello, you must be the Lyons."

Avery spoke up first. "Yes, I'm Avery and this is Peter."

"Please call me Jane. Won't you come in and have a seat?"

Jane Sizemore's office reminded Avery of the small library in St. Charles where she would go to get away from the phone so she could get some studying done in high school. The oversized desk Jane sat at was in front of a large paned window with ceiling to floor bookcases on either side of the window. The floor was of wide plank hardwoods with a red Persian rug under the desk and two Queen Anne, green leather chairs facing the desk.

Avery and Peter sat in the massive chairs and uncomfortably squirmed a little, neither of them confident about the outcome of their visit today.

"Well, Peter, let's start with you. What are the names and ages of your children and what are your concerns about them?"

"Hunter is nine and a-half and Jason is five and a-half. I just think that Avery is handling things wrong. If I need to take her to court to get custody of the kids, I will."

"What kind of things and why do you think it might be necessary to go back to court the get the boys?"

"Well, Avery has had a babysitter 12 times since our divorce was final. I think the children should be at home with her instead of being with a baby sitter all the time. Then, my sister told me that when she drove carpool to school that Avery had the kids half dressed and that they ran out to the car with cereal bars instead of a real breakfast. I don't think that is good for them. She also told me that Avery let Hunter stay by himself while she went to the store and now, I hear that she left them in the car asleep when she went to a party at her friend, Lisa's house. I talked to Hunter's teacher and she says he is behind in his reading and math. And another thing, we both promised each other that we would not bring a string of men and women around the kids until we were serious about someone and Avery has been dating a guy and bringing him around the kids all the time."

"How long has it been since your divorce was final?"

"It was final the last week in November."

"Peter, I'm sure that you both have the best interest of your children in mind. I need to have Avery tell me her version of this now. Go ahead "Avery, what is bothering you?"

Avery was fighting to keep her composure during Peter's ramblings. She was proud of herself for being able to keep her mouth shut while Peter had his say but without hesitation she was very glad to finally get to tell her version. She had promised herself that for the sake of the children she would keep her cool at all costs and abide by what the child psychologist suggested.

"Well, Jane, to answer all of Peters fears, first of all, I have had a babysitter twelve times since our divorce but three of those times my mother babysat for me and one of those times was when a friend's husband died and two of those times my sisters were in town and they were with their cousins who babysat so, I have paid a sitter seven times and several of those times were when Peter couldn't or wouldn't stay with them. Then about sending the kids to school half dressed and without breakfast, I feel that I am guilty of maybe not getting them up soon enough to get ready for school and finish breakfast, but it doesn't seem to matter how early I get them up, they are slow in the mornings. I fix them eggs or pan cakes every morning and milk and juice and they fool around. Sometimes if I feel like they haven't eaten enough so I send them out with a cereal bar too. I always have them dressed. Jason didn't have his shoes tied the last time Lana picked them up for school. I did leave Hunter and Jason in the car asleep when I ran over to my friend Lisa's house. She had just called and told me her husband died. I called Peter to see if he could come get them and he couldn't so I called my sitter to come get them. It certainly was not a *party* and I checked on them every few minutes. I did leave Hunter home for fifteen minutes while I went to the Quickie on Barrow Road to grab some milk. It was a really big deal to him for me to trust him to be big enough to stay by himself since Lana, Peter's sister lets her little girl stay at home by herself often. I showed him how to call 911 if a fire or anything happened while I was gone and made him promise not to cook anything and not to answer the door.

Was that wrong? Oh, and I have also talked to Hunter's teacher. She told me he is behind in his reading too, and I promise you, I do homework with him every night and have him read upstairs in bed, but sometimes when we have a basketball game or soccer game late, I help him do his work in the mornings. I know he is very smart, but I also know that he has had a lot to contend with this year and he needs love, not to be badgered about his grades that are wonderful anyway! About bringing the man I am dating around the children. How can I date without my children around? I really care about this man and I want to have him around the boys to see if it could work out or not. I am not bringing a string of men around them. I have the children twenty-four hours a day except every other weekend and sometimes on Wednesday nights. It's easy for Peter; he has the children so seldom."

"How old did you say Hunter is?" Jane's face was expressionless.

Peter and Avery both in unison said "Nine and a half."

"And what are his grades on the report card showing?" Again, she gave no hint of what she was thinking.

This time Avery answered. "On his last report card he had five A's and a B."

"What about friends, do they both have many friends?" Jane inquired of Avery.

"They both have tons of friends and spend the night our regularly and they both have friends over about two or three times a week. They seem well liked by all of their classmates."

"Peter, do you get that impression as well?" Jane turned her attention to him.

"Yes, they have tons of friends. That isn't the problem."

Jane looked at Peter and Avery with a knowing look. She focused her attention on Peter as she told them, "Peter and Avery, I am not here to point fingers, I am here to tell you what my conclusions of the problems might be, and quite frankly, I see no real problems here with Hunter or Jason. You both must learn that you are divorced now and you cannot control what Avery does while she has the children just as she can't control what you do when you have the children. Hunter and Jason both will have some adjustments to make this year with their would changed so drastically. That is to be expected with a divorce. Now, I know where Barrow Street Quick Pick is and I feel that Hunter is plenty old enough to stay by himself for a short period of time to learn a little independence. I also don't think that Avery has had too many babysitters. If she has had a babysitter twelve times since your divorce, that is an average of one time a week. Hunter and Jason both sound like they are well rounded children. I believe that if you continue to encourage homework time and help him, that Hunter will catch up with his reading and math soon enough.

Peter, you are going to have to remember that while the boys are in Avery's care, you have no control over them anymore. It is evident that you both love your children very much and have their best interests at heart, so I suggest to you that you and Avery are going to have to quit sweating the small stuff and try your best to get along. It is a proven fact that children from divorced parents do almost as well in life as children with non- divorced parents, IF the divorced parents truly make the effort and get along with each other. It is important that you at least act like friends for the sake of your children.

Now, about the dating, as long as neither of you have another person spend the night, there is nothing you can do about that either. No court in the world will take the children away from the custodial parent unless you can prove abuse or co-habitation or drug use. And, understand this, it would be next to impossible for the custodial parent to date without the children knowing about it or being around it. Do either of you have any questions?"

"No, I don't think I do."

"Peter, how about you?"

"No, I don't guess so."

"Well, I wish the both of you the best of luck. It was very nice to meet you and your children sound wonderful. They are going to be fine with time, I assure you. They really do have a couple of great parents."

"Thank you." Avery shook Jane's hand as Peter walked out of the door.

Peter waited for Avery at her car. "She can't possibly know what is going on in our lives, Avery! Just because she seemed to side with you, doesn't mean that she is right!"

"Look, Peter, you are the one who made this appointment. Please remember what she said. You cannot control me anymore. You're the one who made that choice!"

Avery got in her car and didn't look at Peter as she pulled out of the parking lot. Avery found herself feeling like the session with the child psychologist had given her a lift. She couldn't wait to call Grant and give him the news.

"Grant, are you busy?"

"Hey Princess, not at the moment."

"I just had to call and tell you that I feel so empowered after the session with the child Psychologist. She directed her focus directly on Peter and told him that he was going to have to realize that he could not control me, or what I do with the children when I have them. Unless I was to abuse them or something." I really liked her; her name is Jane Sizemore. Do you know her?"

"Can't say that I do. But I am so happy that you are an empowered woman now. I knew that anyway!"

"I'll let you go, I have to pick the boys up later and then I'm headed to St. Charles. Have a great weekend with your boys."

"Hey, be checking your e-mail. I am going to miss you terribly."

"Me too, miss you that is! I will e-mail you too."

"I love you Avery, be careful."

"I love you too, my handsome prince." Avery hung up the phone giggling. It was so great to be around someone who had a sense of humor!

Avery shifted the gears into second on her Ford Expedition as she turned off of the highway onto the lane leading up to the top of the hill to her parent's home. It had been a quiet three hour drive with the boys in the back seat watching the Disney movie, Davy Crockett most of the way. Ever since Jimmie had introduced the boys to Cowboys and Indians and told them of their ancestry relating them directly to one of the Indian chiefs of the Choctaw Nation, Moshulatubbee, they had a great love affair with any movie having to do with Cowboys and Indians, especially, Davie Crockett.

Each year Jimmie and her daughters took all of the children on a "MeMe Vacation." This past summer they had all gone to dig for diamonds in Murphysburrough, Arkansas. Then they traveled to a nearby ghost town to visit a Choctaw Indian burial mound. The grandchildren were in awe of actually getting to peer down into the graves of ancient Choctaw Indians. The trip had heightened their sense of history and of their own heritage.

The last streach of pavement to her mother and father's home was a winding lane lines on both sides with tall, live oaks on either side. Their enormous branches reached across the road to touch each other. White rail fences with horses grazing in front of stately homes gave that restful, calming effect to Avery and excited the boys. At the top of the hill, she turned off the lane into the drive- way also lined with oak and hickory trees and a fence of white spirea bushes draped the driveway in front of the trees. The long driveway circled through a patch of woods and curved in front of the white two-story, colonial house with large white columns on the front porch. In the summer, old fashioned roses, weeping cherry trees, tall spikes of hollyhock, and thick, pink azalea bushes surrounded the white two story and red brick house giving the appeal of a new English Manor.

Avery started honking her horn to announce her arrival. Both boys jumped out of the car and ran up the brick steps to the front door. Jimmie came running to the front door to greet them. The little boys cried "MeMe!" while giving their grandmother a big hug and ran across the shiny hardwood floors of the formal living room into the cozy open kitchen's hearth room to find their grandfather in his recliner, where they knew he would be. Jimmie helped Avery unload the car while Bill played with the boys.

"I am so happy to see you guys! I have some homemade soup on the stove, of course there are hot dogs for the boys."

"Thanks Mom, they shouldn't be hungry, I stopped on the way out of Baton Rouge at McDonald's, but I would *love* some of your homemade soup."

"Great! How was the trip?"

"It was really nice. I had my brain all to myself for once, the kids were into Davy Crockett."

That evening Jimmie and Avery put the boys to bed downstairs in their own quarters. Jimmie was using the den in the walkout basement for her home office. There she had two large, curved desks of rich cherry wood on each side of the room with a computer on one for her and on the other a computer for Liza who worked out of Jimmie's home with her. The walls of the den and office were painted a dark forest green with a touch of yellow that matched the green and navy plaid wallpaper in the bath with a border of golfers around a green golf course. At the other end of the den, sprigs of green grass and budding trees and shrubs were evidence of spring to be enjoyed through the glass windows across the wall. Even with the large desks in the den, there still was room for a tall cherry file cabinet, a copier and a small table and chairs where customers could come in and sign contracts or paperwork. The mother-daughter team sold a lot of real estate from the den in that basement.

The three bedrooms and bath were furnished for overnight company. Each boy had his own room, one with a twin bed and the other with a double pull-out couch, where they usually slept together, and Avery had a room all to herself that was decorated from her teen years at home with a burgundy comforter sprinkled with large beige roses and drapes to match.

Avery said to her mother as they tiptoed from the boy's room, "I think I am going to bed too, Mom."

"Great, Baby, you need to rest and tomorrow Piper, Liza, and the kids are coming over for a big breakfast of bacon and eggs and then Piper is planning to take the boys to her ranch to fish and ride horses with Sagely and Matthew. Liza's kids are at their dad's this weekend."

"Oh, that sounds wonderful. Why don't we go to the ranch with her?"

"We'll see, what ever you want to do. I just want you to relax this weekend all you can."

"I love the ranch. We can relax there, ok, Mom?"

"That's fine with me."

"Thanks, Mom. Goodnight, I love you. Oh, is it OK if I use your computer before I go to bed?"

"Well, of course! Just please don't stay up too late. I really want you to get a good night sleep."

"I promise, goodnight, Mom."

"Goodnight, sweetie."

Avery couldn't wait to check her e-mail. She felt a little silly knowing that Grant probably had not had a chance to write to her yet but excitement ran through her veins at the thought that just maybe he had.

> From: gljclinic
> To: Avery
> Subject: Hi
>
> Hello, my beautiful empowered Princess
> I miss you already! I have had to dig up some daydreams of you. It wasn't hard. I am still on cloud 9 after Wed. night. Thank you for staying with me and for all of the surprises.
>
> The boys and I are going to go hiking tomorrow somewhere, I don't know where yet. When I get to the top of a mountain I will think of you. You make me feel like I am on top of a mountain all

of the time anyway. I'll go now and get some sleep. I'm going to dream of you tonight; will you join me on my cloud?

I love you, GJJ
From: Avery
To: GLJclinic
Subject: Hi
Hey, my sweet Georgia man,

I am in the clouds too! You haven't see me cause I'm up on 10. Let's meet on 11 and I won't be wearing any panties, OK? The trip here was nice and after the meeting with Jane I am ready for a rest. Have a great time with the boys tomorrow and I will call you later, in fact, I am going to call you right now. Bye, my love, Avery

From: GLJclinic
To: Avery
Subject: dreams

Good morning angel. I never heard the phone ring last night. The boys kept me up late last night. When the boys get up we will go grab a bite of breakfast and head to the mountains. I will call you from the top. You know, you make me feel like I am on top of a mountain every time I am with you and you are driving me crazy about the panties. I can't wait to get to the cloud tonight. Right now I would settle for some of your sweet kisses. Seriously, Avery, I love being with you every second we are together. I can never get enough of you. Thank you for coming into my life. I love you and miss you! GLJ

From: Avery
To: GLJclinic
Subject: dreams

Good morning back to you.

Hope I didn't wake the boys when I called. It was a love impulse! We are getting ready to go to the Ranch to ride horses today and then we will probably have lunch there at Piper's; maybe take the kids to see a movie. They have their own movie theater in their house but the kids like to go **to** the movies; they are all rotten. The family wants me to bring you home with me for a visit. Maybe you could come for Easter this year. By the way, you do say the sweetest things! I am so in love with you, I want to keep you forever! Will you marry me, ha!

Love, Avery

To: Avery

From: GLJclinic

Subject: dreams

Hmmmmmmmmmm, are you serious?

To: GLJclinic

From: Avery

Subject: dreams

Hi handsome,

The kids had a ball on Sagley's pony today. Her name is Patches, she is such a sweet horse and just the right size for the kids! It started raining here around noon so we ended up watching a movie in Piper's movie room after all. They have a regular sized movie screen that covers one whole wall in the theater room. It is awesome. I fell asleep during the movie and had the weirdest dreams. Not at all like the dreams I have in the clouds with you. I was fussing at this man in the park because he was humiliating his child in front of everyone! I was brilliant though, it must have been that new empowered thing trying to come out in me. I like my Grant dreams much better.

Whoa, was I serious? Well, I didn't mean to be serious but I don't know. Several issues would have to come out from behind door #3. For instance:

Favorite Cereal? Favorite sit-com? Who takes out the trash? Mows the grass? Favorite meal? Who grills outside? Do husbands still write beautiful e-mails and take romantic walks and do great surprises? Do husbands stay forever? Do they continue to have fun and play once they are married? If not, then, Hell No! Let's just leave it as I love you! Avery

To: Avery
From: GLJclinic
Subject: dreams

Hi again Beautiful. (inside and out) Have I told you lately that I love you?

I can tell you are spending the weekend with Piper, so many questions! Good questions, though. I will answer some or all of them but then you have to do the same.

Favorite cereal=whatever the boys are eating, usually Frosted Flakes.

Favorite sit-com= Fraizer

Take out trash=guy job

Mow grass=lawn service!

Favorite meal=any when we are together

Who grills=whole family

Do husbands still write beautiful e-mails and do surprises=Absolutely, but it requires a wife who really loves to be surprised and romanced and never thinks it gets "old"…

Do husbands stay forever=good ones do.

Now I have a few for you. What is your favorite way to spend a relaxing afternoon? Suppose you are invited to go on a cruise with your friends on the same weekend as your first wedding anniversary, would you go, or would you stay with your husband to celebrate your anniversary… More later, the hospital called, emergency!

After Avery read her last e-mail she sat silent for a very long time in front of the computer. She was lost in a world of thought. *Grant is such a good man. He is such a wonderful father. I know I love him, but why am I a little frightened about us talking about marriage. I wonder if he would change. All men do after they get married. All women do for that matter too. I guess you have to change. You can't keep the pace up that Grant and I have forever. I love what we have now, but I don't want to be just a girlfriend to him. In fact it is kind of embarrassing to be introduced as "this is my girlfriend". It sounds cheap and even silly at our ages. It would be much better to be introduced as "this is my fiancé." My trouble is that I liked being married. I am the marrying kind, and I think Grant is too. God, I hope so. I would die if I thought he was just wanting a date forever. Of course Daddy always has said why buy the cow when you can get the milk free. I certainly hope Grant doesn't feel that way. I am taking a huge risk, but I really don't think Grant would jeopardize the mental well-being of his children or mine by wanting to bring a string of women around them. I can certainly see myself being married to Grant. I can see myself raising his children and helping Travis and Trent with homework and girls and maybe even teach them how to dance. We would have a great time together. Oh, my God, we are really actually talking about getting married!*

Would I really want to marry Grant Jones? You bet I would! "**Mom!**"

CHAPTER 9

Avery flung herself from the computer chair and bound up the stairs to the kitchen where she heard her mother still rattling around. Suddenly she wasn't tired anymore. Her heart was pounding with excitement and she couldn't wait to get to her mother and tell her what she had just read on the computer.

"Mom!" Oh, my God!" You have got to come down here and read this e-mail I got from Grant. He is actually talking marriage!"

"No way, are you serious?"

"Yes, this time I am. Oh, I said will you marry me just kidding him and he took me seriously, I think. What am I going to do?"

"What do you want to do Avery? Did he actually ask you to marry him over the computer?"

"No, of course not, it's just fun stuff; he is just asking me questions and I am afraid of how to answer them now. I don't want him to think that I want to get married right away, but I certainly don't want to run him off either. Please come down and read this and help me answer his questions."

"OK, this might be fun, ha!"

Back at the computer Jimmie read the e-mails Avery and Grant had just written.

"How cute! I don't think you need to hire the caterers just yet." Jimmie said, laughing.

"Mom, I am just so scared. I really feel that I am in love with him, but it just seems to be moving so fast!"

"Avery, do you want some advice?"

"Duh, Yeah."

"Quit worrying that it's moving so fast. It's not like you are really getting married right now, or even having to make that decision. If he seems like the kind of man you may want to marry, then quit worrying. If he is not the kind of man you would marry, then you are wasting both of your time so break it off."

"He is definitely the kind of man I would like to marry, in fact I really believe he *is* the man I want to marry, just not yet. We have so much in common, similar backgrounds, even religion, but I am scared to death. How do I learn to really trust again?"

"Unfortunately, there are no guarantees in this life. You know, he is probably as afraid as you are. I think the only way you can trust him is to get to know him very well. Tell him how you feel about commitment and let him know what you expect from a relationship. Ask him how he feels about those things. Just talk."

"I'm such an open book already. Some of my friends think I should play games with Grant, like go out with other people and don't call him back sometimes when he calls, you know, the *dating game*, but I just can't do that. We have both been tricked and deceived enough. I couldn't do that to anyone, especially Grant."

"I would hope you wouldn't play those *games* with anyone, we always tried to teach you girls to treat others the way you wanted to be treated; besides, Avery, even if you are an open book, you are real. There isn't a fake bone in your body and if Grant wants to run from you for being open and honest, then he would not have been good for you anyway."

"Mother, do you think it's too soon for him or for me to know if we are really in love?"

"I don't know, baby, I know a couple, well, you know them, Fred, your dad's barber. He and his wife had one blind date and the next morning Fred was shipped out to Viet Nam. They wrote letters for two weeks before he asked her to marry him; they got married the day he came home from Nam. He had only seen her that one night. That was forty years ago and five children later. He still talks about his bride like they're newlyweds."

"Good, God! I thought we were moving fast?"

"Well, personally, I think you would be wise to date someone for at least a year. You know, for the four seasons of the year. Piper told me that when she told John that she thought you were falling in love with Grant, she voiced her concern that she was afraid that Grant might not feel the same about you. She said John looked at her like she was nuts and said "Piper, don't be stupid, I'm sure he is already in love with her, anyone with a brain and a pair of eyes couldn't help but to fall in love with Avery!"

"I love my brother-in-law! In fact I love both of them. Grant would fit in with our family very nicely too. I think he would like John and Ronnie."

"I hope so."

"Mom, what about the boys, Jason already loves Grant, but Hunter is seeming a little resentful saying things like. "Mr Grant is **OK**, but he has a big nose or other silly things."

"How is Grant with the boys?"

"He is really wonderful, he holds Jason on his lap as if he were his own. He brings them surprises. He just generally loves children and of course, Jason adores him! He even talks about Mr. Grant to Peter. That really digs Peter, ha!"

"Well, if he really likes them, they will be able to tell. Hunter is going to be protective of you and of Peter. They can only see the family unit as it was, with you and Peter. With time they will adjust, so be patient with them. Stress to Hunter that you want Peter to be happy, and that it is all right to like Peter's new girlfriend. I think sometimes children feel that they are betraying a parent if they like the other parent's girlfriend or boyfriend. That way, you won't be pushing Grant down his throat, but he will get the picture. Evidently, Grant knows the way to the kid's hearts. They do love surprises. Just be sure that you and Grant include them in some quality and fun times together with you and Grant's children. They will learn to love him too."

"Mom, I have slept with Grant already. I am having some guilt feelings, but I honestly wouldn't have slept with him if I didn't think I was in love. For God sakes, I'm thirty five years old!"

"Avery, God sees what's in your heart."

"Thank you, Mom. I love you so much!" Avery hugged her mother tightly. "Now help me answer his e-mail before he gets home to read it."

"OK, this might be fun!"
To: GLJclinic
From: Avery
Subject: Dreams

Hope the emergency was not a serious one, and I hope you don't have to be up all night. I need you to get your handsome rest! Now to answer your questions:

What to do on a lazy Sunday afternoon? (I suppose that is what you meant since Sunday is the only day you ever get to be lazy)

Version #1: With kids: Well, we would wake up to the birds singing, make wild passionate love, then all six of the kids would come in and jump in bed with us and watch Sponge Bob. I would leave you with the whole bunch and fix a big breakfast of bacon, eggs, biscuits, beignets, and coffee.

Then, I would clean up some of the mess while you read the paper and the children will be sent off upstairs to get dressed for church. (all by themselves, of course and perfectly groomed) You and I would then have to hop in the shower together. (not enough time for two showers) After church we would come home and watch ballgames or movies or play video games while we all cuddle on the couch. Later we would work out in the flowerbeds and grille outside and drink some wine.

Version #2: Without the kids: I would wake you up with tiny little kisses. When *we finally decided* to get out of bed, I would cook a great breakfast for you. You could read the paper to me while I was curled up in your lap. We would either go to church or we could read from the bible. We could then cuddle up on the couch to watch a game on TV, or read, or we could decide it was time for a nap (big smile on my face) Then we could plant some new flowers in the garden, afterwards we would go take a hot bath together and I would scrub your back. It would be a wonderful day.

The 1st – 50th wedding anniversary? Let me see, Janie and my friends on a cruise or my handsome, romantic, boss of the universe…thinking, thinking, thinking..Hands down, ALWAYS YOU!"

I love you.

To: Avery
From: GLJclinic
Subject: love quiz

I'm back. Not too bad of an emergency.

Hey, you answer questions really well. I have quite a few more. I especially loved the six kids one. Where did they all come from, anyway?

Okay, more questions.

1. How do you fix a disagreement between husband and wife?

2. Which side of the bed is the husbands and which is the wife's?

3. Which holidays do you spend with in-laws, if the choice is required?

4. Suppose husband accidentally puts a scratch on wife's new car. How does wife respond?

5. How does a husband deal with really, really bad PMS?

6. How does a newlywed couple decide on which church to go to?

7. Suppose husband wants to massage, kiss, and caress, and make love to wife until she is a total noodle and wife wants to do the same to husband. How do you solve this terrible dilemma?

8. How do you keep romance alive forever?

I love you
To: GLJclinic
From: Avery
Suvject: love quiz

You have some very valid questions and I have some very valid answers for you.

1. How to fix a disagreement= Talk about it, try to see **wife's side**, if you can't then compromise… then make love.

2. Husband's side of the bed= is where the new nightstand is, with most talented hand on the side closest to wife.

3. Holidays w/ in-laws= One year his, one year hers, third year invite both to theirs.

4. Scratch on wife's new car= Like she would notice one? If she *would* happen to notice one, she would certainly understand how accidents happen and she would love and kiss him to make him feel better for doing it.

5. Really bad PMS= He would tell her how thin and fetching she looks in that bathrobe, with matted and uncombed hair, and he would bring her a surprise.

6. Which church to go to= visit some and see which one both like, making sure the neighborhood was nice enough that her new car wouldn't get keyed in the parking lot.

7. The massage, kiss, make love till the noodle thing= this is really hard! Hmmmm thinking, thinking, Oh, I know, they should massage each other at the same time, kiss each other and make love till they are *both* noodles!

8. How to keep romance alive= Well, they would have to work at it, try to think of nice things to do for each other, write nice e-mails everyday, surprise each

other occasionally, not wear panties sometimes, and ALWAYS PLAY AND HAVE FUN TOGETHER! *And* make love on an elevator!

And finally, my grandfather told my mom to never let the sun go down without resolving an argument; to kiss your husband or wife everyday before work and when you get home, to say I love you often and for the wife to be a chef in the kitchen and a HO in the bedroom! (Ha! He was born in 1902 so I guess women were either in the kitchen or bedroom at all times)

I love you and I hope the best for this cute little couple, of course, they should get to know each other really well before they make that commitment. I'll be home tomorrow night around 8:00; see you soon, I miss you! Love, Avery

Sunday morning Jimmie, Bill, Avery and the boys went to 8:00 am Mass at the old family church by the river. The day was going to be another spring like, glorious day. After Mass they came home and Jimmie fixed a large brunch of Plain Perdu, eggs and fruit. The boys loved the Perdu, an old family favorite of broken pieces of French bread soaked in egg and milk and fried to a golden crisp. The more syrup and brown sugar on top, the better! Avery and the boys changed clothes and slipped into jeans and sweatshirts and headed for the woods beside the house. They had a great time building a new fort and a fire pit for roasting marshmallows later in the afternoon. The live oaks and tall hickory trees were stripped of all leaves with new buds promising to burst open. The sun streaked through the empty branches leaving shadows that lined the ground like long sections of dark rope. The grounds sloped toward a large fishpond on the property, so all materials for the fort construction had to be carried either up or down hill.

Around five, Avery loaded the exhausted little boys in the Expedition, kissed her mother and father goodbye and headed back to Baton Rouge. The passengers were tired, but happy and the early part of the drive home was chatter about how this spring they were going to do more to their fort and how they would probably even spend the night in it this summer, but only if PaPa had caught that bear he told them was out there. Avery's thoughts were on other things.

*I wonder how seriously Grant was thinking of marriage? That is such a compliment to me, especially since he and his last girlfriend broke up because he didn't want to get married. **Or,** does he just think that **I** want to get married. Is he going to run now because the M word came up. What if I do get married again and it happens again, what if he cheats on me? I still can't figure out what caused Peter to cheat on me. I made myself into the mold of just exactly the kind of wife he wanted me to be, I never even said no to him and **he still cheated**! How in the hell do you know if someone will be faithful? I wish I knew. I just wish I knew. Well, **I** am certainly not going to mention* *the M word again. I will never mold myself to fit anybody else's idea of what I **should** be. If he doesn't like me the way I am I wouldn't want him! I have got to quit worrying, Grant is fun and thoughtful and romantic, I am just going to enjoy this ride as long as it lasts! As Scarlet would say, "I'll just worry about that another day."* Avery smiled as she drove past the stately old Stanton Hall in Natchez.

Avery pulled her car into the carport around 8:30 that evening. She got the boys to bed and started unpacking their overnight bags and sticking the dirty clothes in the washing machine. She drew a hot bath for herself and soaked her stiff muscles from the tiring day and drive. After a long and luxurious bath, she tied her hair up in a new white towel, put on her warmest flannel pajamas and her long, yellow, and terrycloth robe. She moved through the house turning off lamps when she noticed the light blinking on her answering machine.

"Hey beautiful girl. It's around 9:45 and I've been out with a friend. Can't wait to see you. I am going to swing by your house to see if you made it home yet. I can't reach you on your cell. If you get this message and you are tired or something, call and head me off, OK?"

Oh, my gosh! Let me see, it's 10:00. He will be here any second! Avery dashed into her closet and tried to find anything cute to wear. She was not ready for him to see her in her flannel pajamas! She was too late. Grant knocked on the door before she could unbutton her shirt.

"Oh, well, this is the real me. If this doesn't fit his mold, too bad, but I really wish I had on something a little more flattering!

"Hey, I just heard your message, can you tell?"

"I have never seen you look so beautiful!"

"Now I know, you are a liar!" Avery laughed at him.

"I mean it, your skin is so pretty without makeup. I didn't say I had never seen you look more *fashionable*, ha!"

"Come in, Grant. Let me fix us some hot tea."

"Sure you're not too tired." Grant himself was tired. He sat down on a bar stool at the bar in Avery's kitchen and rested his chin on his hand while he watched Avery brewing the tea. He must have drifted off for a few seconds because he thought he heard his youngest son's voice say in that same soothing, girlish voice. "Dad, do you want tea? Do want your tea hot or cold? Dad." He unconsciously waved his hand at his small son and smiled. Then drifted back to Avery's conversation.

"….., and I am so glad you came by. I really missed you! The boys and I made a fire pit to roast hot dogs and marshmallows and I put a wooden bench by the fire pit under this huge live oak tree for us to sit on and make out when you come for a visit. I want you to come home for Easter with me if you can."

"I bet I can."

Avery poured the tea into large mugs and filled them half full, making room for some heavy cream and sugar. She handed Grant his cup and took him by his free hand to lead the way into her living room where she lit the gas logs of the fireplace and they both sat on the couch with hands clutching the large mugs of tea for warmth.

Grant was the first to speak, "I loved the e-mails from your mom and dad's house. You know, I love a big family. Where did you say we got those **six** children?"

"Why, didn't you know, of course, we are going to have twin baby girls!"

"I do believe I would love that! So, four boys and two girls, yep, that makes six."

"And they would have big round eyes and beautiful full lips, just like their father and they would be brilliant, just like their mother!" Avery laughed at her joke.

"Seriously, Avery, I really would love to have twins, but having twins is really hard on the mother. I would worry terribly about you."

"Oh, Dr. Grant, you are way too kind. I bet after having those two big ole boys, a couple of little girls would be a breeze."

Grant laughed at Avery, this time. "Did you know my brother has twins?"

"No, I didn't, there are a lot of things I don't know about you."

"Well, he does, and they are darling; a boy and a girl. I have volunteered my babysitting services any weekend. They really are the cutest things you have ever seen. It's just too bad that they live so far away."

"Well, Dr. Grant, my father's grandmother was a twin and had twins, does that make me eligible?"

"If my memory serves me right from medical school, I believe it does, ha, but just for safety sake, lets ask a good OBGYN."

"My sister, Liza was pregnant with twins, but she lost one of the twins in a miscarriage. Isn't that strange? Oops!" Avery spilled a couple of drops of her tea on her couch and a small amount on Grant's pant leg. "Oh, Grant, I am so sorry!" Avery dabbed at the spill spots with the bottom corner of her pajama shirt.

Grant laughed at Avery. "If we *do* have a *girl* we will have to name her Grace, after you."

"Very funny, Grant." Avery laughed at his joke. "Now, back to the twins. Have you ever heard of miscarriage of only one twin?"

"Yea, I know it happens, especially if the twins are fraternal. Avery, you are so fun, I hope you know that you are the kind of person I have been searching for in my heart all of my life. Another of your e-mails said something about getting to know each other really well, I want that for us, I want to learn everything about you and I want you to know me too."

Grant started kissing Avery on her neck below her ear. She loved his soft kisses; he knew just where to place them to turn her into a mass of putty. She turned to kiss his lips. The kiss was a deep, long and passionate kiss, Grant's breathing became heavy and he searched for her inside of her flannel shirt. He held her close and kissed her until the towel fell from her head.

"Ahhhhhh!" Avery screamed softly and grabbed at her towel and quickly wrapped it around her hair and tied it to her head again. Grant laughed at her antics.

Just then Grant's cell phone rang. "Hello."

"Grant, where are you?" Tara's voice at the other end of the line irritated him with her question, and Grant wondered why she was calling so late.

"I'm at Avery's, why?"

"What are you over there for?"

"Well, Tara, I just am. Why are you calling so late?"

"Are you spending the night over there, or what?" Tara's question was more of a demand than a question.

"No, not that it is any of your business,"

"Well, I would certainly hope not! Your poor judgment just slays me sometimes!"

"Tara, what do you want?"

"I want you to come pick up the boys, or do you think you can **drag** yourself away from your little girlfriend's house long enough to do something for your sons!"

"Tara, I'm going to hang up if you don't quit it!"

"Quit what? I'm just being honest, you don't seem to care about anyone but yourself lately, you are putting that whore ahead of your sons!"

Grant hung up the phone. Avery could see that he was upset.

"What did she want, Grant, is everything alright with the boys?"

Grant's phone rang again. "Hello."

"If you hang up on me again, you will not get the boys this weekend!"

"Then tell me what you want."

"I need you to take the boys to school for me in the morning, do you think you can drag yourself away to do that?"

"Yes, Tara, I will pick them up in the morning."

"Thank you!"

Grant hung up the phone and turned to Avery. "She just wants me to take the kids to school for her in the morning."

"Oh, you are so nice. I can't imagine Peter coming over to pick the boys up for me. In fact, when he has the kids on Wednesday nights he drops them over here early in the mornings so that *I* can take them to school."

"That's hardly fair."

"I know, but that is how it is."

Avery sensed uneasiness in Grant's face. Sudden he seemed very tired.

"I better go."

Avery laughed at herself and tried to make light of what had just taken place. She pulled her clothes together. "That's right! I would hate for you to lose control of yourself over this wet hair do of mine!"

Grant barely smiled. He kissed Avery lightly on her cheek and walked to the door.

"Grant, are you OK?"

"Sure, why?"

"I just don't want you to let Tara make you feel guilty about what kind of parent you are. You are really a wonderful father, in fact, much better than most."

"Oh, she just gets a little crazy sometimes. I think she is having trouble in her relationship with Paul, so she takes it out on everyone else."

"I'm sorry. It is tough to deal with the meatheads sometimes, huh?"

"Yeah. I better go, I'll call you tomorrow." At that, Grant walked out of the door and left to go home.

Avery felt a little sick at her stomach. She hated to see Grant hurt and visibly, Tara was able to get to him.

Avery had a hard time getting to sleep that night. She couldn't get the phone conversation between Grant and Tara off of her mind. *We were having so much fun until Tara called.*

I wonder what she said that made Grant hang up on her? I wonder what she said that made him seem so depressed. They have been divorced for over two years. Why does he let her get to him so badly? His whole demeanor changed after she called. Could he still have feelings for her? After all, she is the one who wanted the divorce. She is the one who had the affair. I certainly don't have feelings for Peter, and he can put me in a bad mood too. I guess that is it. When they attack you for your parenting skills, it just does get to you.

The next morning after taking the boys to school, Avery came home to clean the house and pay some bills. Grant called around ten o'clock.

"Hey, how about letting me drop by your house for lunch today?"

"Well, sure! I'll fix you something yummy."

"I'm not sure what time I will be there exactly. I have a patient scheduled for a stress test in a few minutes. I should be finished around 12:30 or 1:00."

"What ever, I will be home all day."

"Great, I'll see you then; love you."

"I love you too."

Avery hung up the phone and her mood immediately lifted. Grant sounded like he was in a much better frame of mind this morning.

Avery straightened up the house and ran out to get some turkey pocket sandwiches from the neighborhood deli. She decided deli sandwiches would be much better than the peanut butter she had in her pantry or the cheese and crackers she normally ate for lunch at home.

Grant pulled in the driveway around 1:30. It never bothered Avery if he was late. She actually accepted it as Grant's job and way of life, and besides, she was late for almost everything. She had made her mind up that she was going to have to learn to quit trying to crowd so many things into her life in such a short time period, or at least to say no to some of those things that bogged her life down.

Avery walked outside and met Grant on the back patio.

"Hey, boss of the Universe!"

"Hey there, Princess!"

"Boy, I have gone all out fixing a great lunch for you!" Avery teased.

"Anything sounds great, I am starved!" The two walked with their arms around each other's backs into the back door of Avery's house. Grant pulled a chair out from the round table sitting by the windows of the kitchen where Avery had set two colorful place settings. The sun felt warm streaming into the window-lined kitchen, for a February day. Avery served the sandwiches and sat down with Grant at the table.

"How did the test go?" Avery asked lifting the turkey sandwich to her mouth.

"Good, the man may have a little blockage, we will have to do more testing to be sure. Guess what?"

"What?" Avery smiled at Grant her curiosity was peeked. Grant took the last bite of his sandwich and Avery waited patiently while he chewed and swallowed.

"Well, Friday is Valentine's Day, and in my family, it isn't just Valentine's Day, it's Valentine's Week. I have a little something for you and with each day the surprises get a little better."

Grant pulled a small box from his pocket and held it out to Avery.

"How sweet! I can't believe you did this!"

"Well, you better open it before you get too excited. It is very small."

Avery took the lovely little box that was wrapped in red foil paper with a white ribbon. She excitedly opened it, but slowly enough to make the surprise last.

"Oh, Grant! How lovely!" You are the most wonderful guy in the whole world! I love surprises!"

"Universe."

"Yeah, the most wonderful in the Universe!" Avery laughed at Grant.

Inside the box were double stacked, bite-sized chocolates from Neiman Marcus. Avery took a small bite off of a piece of the chocolate candy. "Oh, my God, Grant, you have to try these." Avery fed him the rest of her piece of chocolate. Then Grant took one and fed it to Avery. They kissed as they sucked on the chocolate candy and giggled. "I have to get back to the office, walk me to the car, I have something for the boys too. You can give it to them when they get home from school."

"Grant, you are full of surprises. The boys will be so thrilled! I love you for thinking of the boys and I love Valentine Week! Thank you!"

Avery was touched that Grant had thought of the boys as well as of her. They were going to be so excited!

Every day of Valentine Week was full of shopping for just the right things for Grant and his sons, and every evening was the exchange of Valentine gifts of all sorts. On the evening of Valentine's Day, Grant came to pick up Avery for dinner and brought the boys both movies. She and the boys gave Grant a Polo pull over knit shirt to take to Miami and his favorite bottle of Chablis. Then Grant and Avery left the boys with their sitter and went to a very exclusive restaurant where they enjoyed the ambiance of dimly lit candles and soft music. The waiter escorted them to a table in back of the room by a towering window with a view overlooking the river. They ate a wonderful meal of blackened sword fish and watched the return of the shrimp boats with light bulbs strung up on wires like a carnival rides, coming home from a hard day of work.

"Avery, in a couple of weeks when I meet you in Miami, I want to take you to this fabulous restaurant that is built on a cliff overlooking the ocean. Katie says that the view is really fabulous there. She says that the waves of the ocean break on the rocks and spray the glass with every wave. The food is supposed to be great too."

"I can't wait, we will have such wonderful time! Mom is going to baby-sit for me. She is going to hate me. I looked at the kids schedule and they have a whole week end of ball games, I hope Peter helps her with all of that!"

"I bet he will, after all, he wants your family to think he is still a great guy doesn't he?"

"Yes, you are right, unless, of course he has other plans. I'll ask Mary Beth to help her. She will be at all of the same games too."

After dinner Grant took Avery back to his house. They poured a glass of wine and Avery settled herself on the couch while Grant excused himself to the back part of the house. He was carrying a large box wrapped in an expensive white on white gift-wrap and an enormous white bow with a single pink rosebud in the center.

"Oh, Grant what have you done! This is absolutely gorgeous!"

Grant smiled in anticipation.

"This is for the Miami trip too."

Avery opened the box and there she found a beautiful assortment of candles, bath oils, body rubs and aromatherapy bath salts.

"Oh, my gosh! You are so much fun. We will definitely put all of this to good use!" She grabbed and kissed him, laughing all the while until they both fell over on the couch. They lay facing each other on the small couch. Grant looked deeply into Avery's eyes. She looked slightly different tonight. Her almond shaped eyes were the same her beautiful golden skin and hair were the same. She looked a little younger, maybe. He didn't know what was different; maybe it was the way the light was making shadows on her face. Just then he thought he heard her softly say, "Dad."

"Hey, quit staring at me and give me a kiss!" Avery smiling, pulled Grant's face to hers and kissed him passionately."

Miami was fun, Avery and her friends Janie, Rachel, and Joan roomed together in a Holiday Inn on the East End of Miami. A bus shuttled them from the hotel to the tennis tournament and was available every hour for convenience. The first morning as the girls were stirring in their beds, they heard a knock. "Room Service." Someone said at the other side of the door. Janie bounced out of bed and opened the door.

The bellboy pushed a cart full of every kind of breakfast treat the hotel menu had available. "My God!" Janie screamed. "You all have got to get up and look at all of this! There are even diet cokes for me!" Janie was veraciously going through all of the covered dishes on the trey. "Avery, look! Here is a card. It says, *I hope you girls have a great time, Love Grant.* "Damn, Ave, what did you ever do to deserve this guy?"

Avery jumped out of bed and ran over to look at the beautiful array of foods followed by Rachel and Joan.

"I'm telling you guys, he stepped right out of a romance novel, he isn't real!" Avery told the girls as they ooed and aahed.

Avery immediately called Grant on his cell at the Baton Rouge Heart Clinic.

"Grant, you doll! Do you hear the girls in the background? They are scavenging this beautiful cart of food you had sent to the room. How in the world did you think of something so nice?"

"Gee thanks, Grant." Janie yelled

"Yea, Thank you!" Rachel and Joan yelled

Rachel then yelled over Avery into the phone, "If you see that no-good husband of mine at the hospital today, tell him to get his ass in gear and do something nice for us too!"

Rachel's husband was a orthopedic surgeon and Grant occasionally ran into him during the course of the day.

"Grant, I know you are busy, I just had to call and thank you. I can't wait till you get here. I will leave here day after tomorrow and check into our hotel at Southbeach and wait for you there."

"Sounds great, I'll be in around 6:00 pm. It seems like you have been gone forever!"

"I have been gone forever! I love you.

"I love you too, bye and be careful."

"Ok, bye."

"Throw up, for God's sake! You two are sickening!" Janie and the girls couldn't help but tease Avery.

The third and final day of the tennis tournament finally came. Avery was full of excitement thinking that Grant would be here soon. After Janie, Rachel and Joan left to catch their plane back to Baton Rouge, Avery packed, checked out and caught a taxi to Southbeach where she checked in under Grant L. Jones reservation. The bell captain took her bags up the elevator to the fourth floor suite that she would be sharing with Grant for the rest of the week.

Avery unpacked the things she brought for this part of her trip and put them neatly into one of the drawers of the elegant armoire. She pulled out the candles and bath salts and arranged them in the bath. The suite was luxuriously appointed with massive cherry furniture. A king sized bed with four posters, the ornate armoire and a matching dresser with a ceiling to surface mirror in gilded gold were tastefully arranged on one end of the large room and at the other end of the room, in front of a glassed wall next to sliding glass doors that let to a private balcony, was a small sitting area with a beige leather love seat, two overstuffed, chairs in a plaid fabric that matched the colors in the floral print bedspread. In the center of the sitting area was a cocktail table with fresh flowers. Avery surveyed her surroundings and went to the bathroom to take a shower and wash her hair. Her thoughts were spinning. *This is the first time in my life I have ever stayed in a hotel with a man, besides Peter, in my life. I wish I weren't so nervous. What should I be doing when he gets here? Maybe I'll be on the balcony waiting with a cocktail in my hand. That would make me seem very sophisticated! Or, maybe I will put on my bikini and be laying out on the balcony, hmmmm.*

Avery finished blow-drying her hair and searched through the clothes she had hung on hangers in the small closet in the bathroom. She chose a casual, black, soft knit dress with a plunging neckline and spaghetti straps. The dress was simple but sexy, showing off her curvy figure. Little string sandals of many colors were all she needed to complete her outfit and a pair of small gold loop earrings to match her delicate gold chain bracelet.

Avery sat on the balcony with a cocktail, choosing the look of sophistication but at 6:15, could sit there no longer. She left the room and caught the elevator down to the lobby. There she spotted Grant at the front desk checking in. She eased up beside him and in a low, husky voice and said "Hey good looking stranger!"

Grant turned to see who was talking to him. At the sight of Avery he grinned broadly, threw one are around her waist and pulled her close while he signed his charge ticket.

"I was trying really hard to be patient and make you see how sophisticated I am by sitting on the balcony with my cocktail, but it just wasn't happening." Avery was laughing at herself.

"I'd rather have you here with me, you look gorgeous!" Grant held her tightly with one arm and lifted his bag with the other hand and they walked arm and arm through the lobby to the elevator.

"Grant, this hotel is fabulous, I can't wait till you see our room!" Avery was visibly excited. "And, I don't have any panties on." She whispered in his ear.

They stepped on the elevator and Grant pushed the button to the fourth floor. He dropped his bag and grabbed Avery with both arms and they kissed until the elevator stopped at its destination. The doors opened to a crowd of people waiting to get on. Avery and Grant calmly stepped off of the elevator and when the crowd entered the elevator they ran laughing to their room.

Grant and Avery spent the next morning strolling hand and hand around Southbeach looking in small shops and stopping occasionally to buy t-shirts for each of their boys. After lunch, they sat by the pool sunning and people-watching while they sipped on gin and tonics. After a romantic dinner at one of the small café's downtown, they strolled hand in hand, barefoot along the beach. They decided to go back to the hotel and take a dip in the pool. It was quiet around the hotel lobby. The other tourists and guests were out enjoying the diverse club scene at Southbeach or out for a late dinner, or in bed already. Grant and Avery didn't have to wait on the elevator doors to open in the lobby. They entered and stood holding hands. Grant pushed the button for the 12ᵗʰ floor. The elevator started the assent upward and Grant grabbed Avery and kissed her passionately. They were like two starved beasts kissing and feeling for each other wildly. Grant pulled Avery around with her back to the elevator controls, he held in the close door button while kissing her. He ran his free hand up her thigh and raised her dress. She wrapped one long, slender leg around him and they made passionate love standing in the elevator.

Part 9

The flight home was wonderful for Grant and Avery. They snuggled on the plane and talked about their plans for the future. They seemed to take it for granted that they would someday be married. Grant told Avery that when he did propose to her that it had to be the most romantic setting in the world. It would have to be on a mountaintop or on the beach with the ocean to their backs at sunset. They agreed that not enough time had elapsed for a respectable couple to get married yet, but it certainly was not too soon to plan and to dream about it.

Grant helped Avery with her bags into her house. Jimmie and the boys were glad to see them. The little boys jumped on their mother and then Jason jumped on Grant. Grant and Avery pulled the t-shirts they had bought for the boys out of a bag and the boys tried them on and ran through the house in excited bliss. Jimmie fixed the tired couple a glass of tea while they told her all about Southbeach in Miami. About the diverse locals and the obvious tourists. They told about their dinner at the cliff restaurant and the beautiful hotel they stayed in. After a short visit, they kissed goodbye and Grant told Avery to come by his house for breakfast after she took the boys to school in the morning. He didn't have to go into the office until noon. Then he left to go see his sons before he went home.

Tara answered the door. "Grant, where have you been all weekend, I have called and called and you obviously had your cell phone turned off."

"Yea, I didn't want to be bothered."

"What if I had an emergency!"

"Tara, you know if you had an emergency that the answering service knew how to reach me."

"Oh, like I have to reach you through the answering service now, like one of your lowly patients!"

"Tara, don't call my patients lowly. They have been paying your bills for years. I don't want to argue with you, I just want to see the boys. Where are they?"

"So, I guess if I want to talk to you I have to make an appointment now! Were you with Avery?"

"That's none of your business. Travis, Trent! Are you guys here?"

"What are you going to do, Grant, *marry* her after knowing her for four whole months? That's what I heard. That you and Avery are already talking marriage! If your patients knew how irresponsible you are they wouldn't be around for long. You can be such an idiot!"

"Who told you that?"

"Oh, let's just say a friend of a friend."

Grant pushed past Tara when he heard the boys bounding down the long spiral staircase that led up to their rooms in the big house. "Hey guys!"

"Dad! How was your trip?" Travis was glad to see his father. He felt that he was too old at eleven to run and jump on him so he slowed down at the foot of the stairs and gave his dad a high five while his younger brother ran full speed not far behind him and jumped into his father's arms.

"It was great, man. I want to take you guys to Miami maybe this summer. It is really a cool place!"

'Yeah! And take us to Disney world again and to Sea World too!" Piped in Trent.

Grant laughed. "We'll see. We will be doing a lot of cool stuff this summer. Hey, I brought you guys something."

"What! What is it?" Both boys danced around excitedly.

"Come with me to the car and I'll get them for you."

The boys were right on Grant's heels as they walked out of the massive front door of the old tutor home.

Grant pretended to ignore Tara as she said, "You should have brought their surprises in the house. It's too chilly for the boys outside. You boys hurry and get back in the house!" she yelled after them.

Grant pulled the t-shirts from his bag and gave each boy his shirt and a baseball hat. "Thanks Dad!" Trent couldn't get his shirt over his clothes fast enough and then put his new hat on over his tousled hair. "How do I look, Dad?"

"Like a real baseball player for Florida!" Grant was pleased that his youngest son liked his gift. About that time, Tara stuck her head out of the door and was yelling at the boys to come in. Trent kissed his dad goodbye and ran to the house. Travis held his shirt and hat in his hand and looked up at his father.

"You know, Dad, you let her get away with way too much."

"What do you mean, Travis?"

"I mean that you let her treat you too bad."

"I don't know what to do about that, son. If it means that I have to put up with her treating me bad to see you guys, then I guess I'll just have to put up with it because no one or nothing is going to keep me from seeing you. I don't think you should have to worry about that though."

"Dad, I just think that you should not even come in the house to see us. Just call and tell us you are coming and we will meet you outside."

"What will stop her from coming outside to raise cane?"

"I don't know, Dad, I just think she wouldn't come outside and yell as much as she yells in the house at you, and one more thing, Dad. She doesn't tell you the truth sometimes."

"What do you mean, son?"

"Well, I have heard her yelling at you on the phone and I've heard her tell you that Trent and I don't like Avery, but we do like Avery, Dad."

"Travis, I know you do. It's just going to take your mother some more time to get used to the idea of me dating and of another woman being around you guys. Try to be patient with your mother but I want you to know that I know how things are. You are not to worry anymore about your dad. I am the king of the universe, remember?"

"Yeah, I remember."

Grant grabbed his son and hugged him tightly.

"Travis! I said get in the house right now!" At Tara's last demand, Travis let go of his father and ran into the house.

Grant was depressed during the short drive home. *Damn it! Why did she have to be such a devil? His heart ached for his sons. What in the hell was I thinking when I married her. My poor sons, especially Travis; she always seems to pick on him the most. He is so young to have to feel my pain. Damn, I hate her! Why in the hell couldn't I have met Avery twelve years ago? Maybe when Avery and I get married the boys will come to live with us. I would hate to hurt Tara, but I bet the boys would love to get away from her sometimes.*

Lately, Grant had been treating Tara as if she didn't exist. He certainly had not been paying the attention to her or giving in to her demands like she was used to. She had always known that she could play on his soft heart to get him to do just about anything she wanted him to do, that is before he met Avery. After she tucked the boys into bed and called Paul, she lay in her bed and began to think. *I'll show Avery Lyons, she probably thinks that Grant is in love with her. She is so stupid. I need to try to get him back. That shouldn't be too hard. I'm pretty sick of Paul's attitude lately. I'll fix her little boat. How dare he go off to Florida with her and not even tell me where he is going! How dare he have her spend the night with him last week when I wanted him to take the boys to school for me! And to think, my children saw her practically naked getting the paper in front of his house that morning!* Tara then got on the phone and started making calls.

The next morning Grant got up early and put on the coffee for his breakfast with Avery. He went back to his bath to shower and shave. He heard the back door open and wrapped a towel around his waist. "Hey, Princess, pour us a cup of coffee and I'll be there in a minute."

Grant finished his shave and went into the kitchen to meet Avery.

"What in the hell are you doing here? Get out!"

"Why Grant, I thought you would *enjoy* seeing me naked in the morning in your kitchen."

"I'm telling you, Tara, get out now. Give me the key and get out!"

Tara came from behind the kitchen counter holding the key to Grant's house up high in her hand. She was totally naked and as she came around the counter she acted sweet and coy in an evil way. She held the key up in front of Grant's face like she was going to give it to him. He reached for the key and she threw her arms around his neck and started kissing him hard on his mouth. He grabbed her by the waist and tried to push her back. She clawed at him like a crazed cat hanging on around his neck and jumping up, wrapping her legs around his hips. He grabbed her arms to pull her off and his towel fell to the floor. He wrestled with her and she managed to pull him on top of her on the couch in the gathering place of the kitchen. Grant was trying to get off of her without hurting her, "Tara, stop it! What is the matter with you? Have you gone crazy? Tara grabbed and clutched him. She wrapped her legs around his body. He couldn't break the hold without hurting her. She released her hold and he managed to roll off of her just as Avery walked in the door.

Avery stood in the door of the kitchen with her mouth open, not able to move, or breathe. Grant jumped up off of the floor and grabbed his towel to cover himself. "Avery, please, it isn't what you think." Grant pleaded as he moved toward Avery. Tara laid back on the couch and put one bare leg up over the back of the sofa. "Grant, darling, you didn't tell me you were expecting company. She said sweetly"

Tears sprang into Avery's eyes; she bolted out of the door and was in her car and speeding out of the driveway before Grant could catch her.

"Get the Fuck out of my house and don't you ever put your sick foot back in here again! Do you hear me Tara?"

"Why, Grant, Don't tell me you didn't want me. Well, guess what, I really didn't want you!"

"Get out before I call the police, Tara! And give me that damn key!"

Tara smiled an evil smile and slowly got up and walked to the kitchen counter where she had laid her trench coat. She took her time and slid it on over her bare body. She strolled to the back door and looked over her shoulder as she said, "I guess you'd rather settle for second best, my darling?"

"Give me the damn key and get out, you witch!"

"Tara tossed the key up in the air and it landed on the floor at Grant's feet as she walked out of the door."

Grant was overcome with grief for Avery's feelings and disgust for Tara. What in the hell had she done to Avery. He was sick at his stomach. He tried to reach Avery on her cell phone. She wouldn't answer. He called her home and left her a message. "Avery, angel, please listen, it isn't what it looked like. Please call me. Please let me explain. I love you. I love you, baby, please call me. Grant began to cry. He hadn't cried real tears since the first time he saw his newborn sons. He quickly went to his room and hastily dressed. He drove to Avery's house. She wasn't there. He went to the office and tried to concentrate on his patients.

After work, he drove to Avery's house again. The house was dark and Avery's car was still gone. Grant went home, sank down on the couch and drank shots of straight whiskey in between futile calls to Avery. He sat on his couch with a bottle to keep him company while the thought. *I know now that Tara is really the devil. I wish I could send her right back to hell where she belongs. My God, Avery! She will never believe in me again! She will never trust me again. She has been so hurt and now she has to be thinking the worst.* Grant sorrow sunk deeper and deeper into the very depth of his soul. *Where in the hell could she be?* Grant didn't remember passing out on the couch. He dreamed fitfully that he was sitting at his desk at the office trying to decipher a lab report and his nurse kept getting in his face. "Dr. Jones, Dr. Jones, you need to get up and eat your lunch. Your people are here and they are waiting for you." *Couldn't she see that he was busy? Why did she have to be such a nag? He wasn't hungry, he needed to be certain of the findings of this lab report before he saw his next patient and his time was running out!* He waved her off with his hand and tried to concentrate on the report. Early the next morning Grant got off of the couch and drug himself to the shower. His head was pounding and the sorrow of what had happened the night before came flooding back to him in nauseas waves. Grant showered and dressed then he went to his computer.

To: Avery @ aol.com

From: GLJclinic

Subject: Please read this.

Dear Avery, PLEASE, PLEASE, READ THIS.

Avery, I was in my towel shaving when I heard the door open in the kitchen. I thought it was you. I walked in and Tara was standing there naked. I told her to get out. She had a key to my house that I had given her when I first bought the house in case the boys needed to come in and get anything while I was gone. I yelled at her to give me the key and get out. She walked over to give me the key and instead she grabbed me and I swear to God, I was wrestling her to get her off of me when you walked in. I am so sorry baby that you had to see that. I hate her! She really is the devil! Please believe me, Avery. It is the God's truth. I love you, and I will understand if you never want to see me again, but I beg you to try to believe me about this. It is the truth. I am so very sorry that you had to see that and that you are hurt! I am sick about that. Please know that I love you with all of my heart and I will never ever love anyone else as long as I live. Please call me if you read this, Avery. Please call me. I am crazy not knowing where you are. I love you more than you will ever know. Grant

Avery could hardly see to drive. She made it to Janie's house and banged on the door. Janie was washing breakfast dishes.

"Janie, I just caught Grant and his ex wife having sex on the couch at his house!" Avery was sobbing.

"No way!" Janie's mouth dropped open.

"Janie, I walked in the kitchen and they were, right there on his couch, both naked!"

"I want to kill that bastard!" Janie was furious.

"When I walked in he rolled off of her onto the floor. I don't understand, he knew I was coming over."

"That bastard!"

The phone rang. "Hello," Janie answered on the first ring.

"Hey Janie, it's Lisa. Listen, I heard something last night that disturbed me."

Avery sat at the bar in Janie's kitchen and Janie poured her a glass of water and handed her a paper towel to wipe her tears while she talked with Lisa holding the phone between her neck and her ear.

"What did you hear?"

"Well, a friend of mine that is a friend of Tara Jones called me and said that Tara had told her last night that she had heard that Avery thought she and Grant might be getting married. She said, that Tara said, that Avery is about the third or fourth girl that he was suppose to marry. That rumors had been flying about a girl Grant was going out with that thought she was suppose to marry Grant and she ended up getting fired from her job and no one knows what happened to her. Obviously Grant didn't get married to her either.

This friend told me that Tara said that Grant pulled this stuff just to make her jealous. That he is still in love with Tara."

"Well, yesterday I would have said that rumor was just a lie from Tara's own imagination. Today, I think it's probably true."

"What makes you say that?" Lisa asked.

"I'll have to call you later. Avery just dropped by."

"Gotcha. Call me later."

"Janie, what am I going to do? I was so much in love with him. I never want to see him again!" Avery sobbed in her hands.

"That slimy creep! How dare he do this to you! Man, you just never know, do you, that bastard! Lisa just called and said that he has told several women that he was going to marry them, I guess you aren't the only one, if that is any consolation."

"Janie, would you keep the boys for a couple of days for me. They can't miss school and I have to go home for a few days. I have to go home to get myself together. I think I am going to have a nervous breakdown! I wasn't this crushed when I found out about Peter's affair!"

"I know, you didn't love that asshole anymore. This asshole had you by the heart and soul. That bastard! Avery, you are so lucky to have such close ties with your family. You go home, the boys will be fine here with me. You go home and let your family help you through this."

"Janie, I'll come back Friday to get the boys and take them home with me or something. Maybe Mom will come back with me. I just have to get away."

"You go girl. The boys will be fine and it's a done deal."

"I love you Janie. You've got Mom's number. Here is the key to my house. I'm going to pack a few things for the boys and I'll bring over what they need. Anything else and you go over to get it, OK?"

"OK. Don't worry we will be just fine. My girls love to play with Hunter and Jason and Jesus, they go to the same school. No big deal!"

"Thanks, Janie."

Avery walked out of Janie's door in a daze and exhausted from crying. There was no feisty sparkle or golden girl, just a very sad and depressed woman that had been hurt one too many times.

Grant was sick with worry. He had not been able to reach Avery even though he had called every half hour between patients. He drove past her house this morning before work and she wasn't there. He drove past her house this evening when he got off, but she wasn't there. He sat alone in the dusk staring out of the window into his back yard drinking his supper. Hard liquor seemed to be the only thing that dulled his senses enough to ease the pain he was feeling. He decided to call Janie. *What in the hell is her last name? Damn!* He felt so helpless! *I know, I will try to call her mother.*

"Information, what city, please."

"St. Charles, I need the number of Bill or Jimmie Lynch, please."

"That number is area code 225-650-4663."

Grant's hands trembled as he dialed the number. His hands didn't tremble when he performed delicate surgery. He was afraid of what he might hear. He knew that Jimmie and Bill Lynch liked him, but to have to tell them what had happened and how it had hurt Avery was something else. *What if she was there and they wouldn't let him talk to her? What if she wasn't there, where could she be?* The knot in his stomach tightened.

"Hello," Grant heard Jimmie Lynch at the other end of the line.

"Jimmie, hello, this is Grant. I hate to bother you but does Avery happen to be there?"

"Well, I'm not supposed to say that she is."

"So, she is there?"

"Yes, but Grant I don't think I can get her to talk to you. She is crushed, you know."

"Jimmie, I know, she has to be. She thinks I was having sex with my ex-wife and I was trying to get her off of me and throw her out of my house. I swear, she is the devil straight from hell! Would you please ask Avery if she will talk to me?"

"Let me go get her, Grant, hold on a minute, Ok?"

Jimmie went out on the deck where she and Avery had been sitting. "Avery, it's Grant, he really wants to talk to you."

"Mother! You told him I was here? I asked you not to tell him where I was if he called!"

"Avery, he says he was trying to throw Tara out of the house when you came in."

"Yeah, right! And I am the Pope!"

"He sounds pretty miserable, won't you at least hear what he has to say?"

"No, Mother! I never want to speak to him again. I saw what he and Tara were doing and I will not listen to any lame excuses or any more lies! I don't need to ever talk to him again!"

"Ok, Ave. I'll tell him."

"Grant, I am so sorry, but Avery will not come to the phone. She said that she saw what you and Tara were doing with her own eyes and no excuses will change that. I'm sorry."

"Jimmie, I understand how she would think that. I swear in God's name that it was not what it must have looked like. Would you please see if you can get her to read my e-mails?"

"Grant, I will try, but I can't promise a thing. She can be a pretty stubborn girl."

"All I ask is that you try. I love her so much, and I am so sorry that she is hurt, even though it wasn't what she thought."

Jimmie thought she heard a faint sob at the other end of the line. "Grant, give her a few days, maybe she will be ready to talk later. I will try to get her to check her e-mail."

"Thank you Jimmie. At least I know she is safe and there with you."

"She'll be fine. Thank you for calling, Grant."

Jimmie didn't quite know what to think. She was pretty good at judging someone's character and Grant seemed to be a very upright young man. She was shocked when Avery came home and told her what she had seen. Maybe Grant had never gotten over his first wife. Maybe he couldn't help himself. It was just too damn bad that it had to be at the expense of Avery and the boys.

Jimmie told Avery that Grant wanted her to read her e-mail.

"You know, Mother, I have gone down this road before. I don't want to read my e-mail. I don't want to hear more lies. Just like Peter, begging me to come back and all the while he was banging his girlfriend. I am not going to listen to anymore shit! I am going to go home and get my sons and I am never going to trust another man as long as I live! I don't need a man, I don't want a man and by God, no man is ever going to hurt me, or my children again! I guess I have always thought there might be someone out there like my daddy, and Mom, I just don't think God made anymore of them."

"Avery, honey, that's just not true. I know you are hurt, but I want you to remember something. Things are not always what they seem."

"Yeah, well this time, I don't see how they could be any other way but what they seem! I am going to be fine, Mother. I'm over the shock, I'm just mad at myself for being such a fool! I will leave tomorrow and go pick up the boys from Janie's. You are welcome to come with me, if you want to."

"I'll see if I can get away for a few days in the morning. Let's go to bed and get some rest.

"Goodnight Mom."

"Goodnight, baby."

The next morning the doorbell rang at 8:30 am. Jimmie was just finishing her make up.

"I'll get it." she yelled to Avery.

Jimmie opened the door to a huge and lovely bouquet of spring flowers of every color. One of the most beautiful she had ever seen.

The local florist delivery lady was standing at the front door with an impatient look on her face as Jimmie gaped at the stunning flowers.

"Is Avery Lynch here?"

"Yes, I'll take them, thank you."

Jimmie hurriedly took the bouquet from the lady, thanked her, and closed the door behind her with her foot. She carried the bouquet into the kitchen where Avery was sitting having coffee.

"Avery, these were delivered for you. Aren't they gorgeous!"

"Yeah, they are. See who they are from, will you, Mom? It has to be Janie or Grant, they are the only people who know I'm here."

"They are from Grant."

"Send them back!"

"Avery, don't you want to read the card?"

"No, Mother."

Jimmie pulled the card out of the flowers and began to read. *"Avery, I know it's hard to believe one thing and to see another; that is the meaning of faith. Please, if you won't talk to me, at least read my e-mail, and if you never want to see me again. I will understand. Just know that I will love you more than my life, forever. Grant"*

"Mother, I don't want to hear that shit!"

"Avery, I have never seen you so hardened. Won't you please read his e-mail. I really think he is sincere."

"Mother, what is he sincere about, that he is in love with his first wife and she won't take him back because she is a spoiled rotten brat and wants to use him and have a boyfriend too and he wants me for a diversion?"

Avery left the room and went downstairs to get her things. She kissed her mother goodbye and left for Baton Rouge.

She felt a little guilty about not asking her mother to come home with her but she knew her mother would badger her to talk to Grant and she couldn't handle that pressure right now.

CHAPTER 10

The next few weeks Avery lived as if she were lost in a fog. She could perform only the most fundamental tasks in her heavily misted world. Exhaustion or her blank mind prevented her from doing anything more than was required for survival for her sons.

She trudged through her routines mechanically, like a robot, with no feeling or meaning to what she was doing. She faked smiles for her sons and pretended to be interested in what they were doing, but their conversations seemed muddled and sounded distant until they faded away completely. That's when she would find herself being pulled back into the dreaded reality by Jason or Hunter yelling "Mom, Mom!" and pulling on her hand or clothing.

She found herself crying at least once a day for no apparent reason, of course, she knew why, but her children didn't understand why their mother was so sad.

She had loved her life and she adored her sons. She had tons of friends and not too long ago thought she could be happy just the way things were. Why then, couldn't she pull herself out of this deep sadness she felt? She had been angry, insulted and embarrassed at Peter's betrayal, but she had not felt like this. The constant and deep sadness was becoming more than she could bear. She understood now how people could kill themselves. Avery knew she had to do something for her children, if not for herself. She called her doctor and made and appointment for herself as soon as she could get in to see him.

She never answered her phones anymore; if anyone wanted to talk to Avery, they had to leave a message. She was afraid of who may call and if it happened to be Grant, she couldn't bear to hear him lie to her. She couldn't imagine what he could possibly say to make what she saw go away or to even make it seem not so bad. She also was so afraid of her own weakness and afraid that she would jump at a chance to believe him and couldn't or wouldn't allow herself the opportunity to be such a fool again.

The boys missed Grant almost as much as she did, especially little Jason. She could not allow anyone else to hurt them. She would never bring a man around her children again. Peter was right about that one. Maybe she would date again when the boys were grown and gone if she wasn't too old or sick.

Thank God, Avery was able to get in to see the doctor a few days after she called for the appointment.

After a thorough examination, the doctor told her to get dressed and that he would be back in the tiny room shortly to talk to her. Avery sat upright on the leather examining table, dressed and trying to focus on a magazine while waiting for the doctor to come back in.

Dr. Ralph had been her doctor since she and Peter had moved to Baton Rouge. He was a general practitioner but had delivered both of her babies. He was an older man, very tall, with graying brown hair at his temples and a fabulous bedside manner. Talking to Dr. Ralph was like talking to a loving grandfather. Not at all like talking to her own father who immediately would have to give her ropes of rambling advice or who would feel compelled to personally fix her problem, himself.

Dr. Ralph had a way about him that made you want to tell him anything.

"Avery, you seem to be in perfect health, a little too thin, but healthy. Do you want to tell me why you felt the need to come in before it was time for your yearly checkup?"

"Well, I hate to bore you with my problems; in fact, I really don't have any problems. I should be so grateful for what I have and for my beautiful children, but I am so miserable."

"That is what I'm here for, Avery. Tell me everything."

Avery began telling him about finding out about Peter's affair, the fact that Peter had been so controlling and mean that she was really happy to get out of the marriage. She told about the ugly divorce, and how hard it is to get along with Peter now. As she began to tell him about meeting and falling in love with Grant, tears began rolling down her cheeks. By the time she told him of the scene she had walked in on, she was sobbing uncontrollably.

Dr. Ralph sat on his small stool in front of her and let her cry. He handed her several tissues but said nothing until Avery started trying to compose herself.

"Avery, I heard that you and Peter had divorced. I always hate to hear of a family breaking up, but personally, I am glad you are out of that relationship. That was not a healthy one for you."

Avery tried to smile at him as she dabbed at her watery eyes.

"You probably have not been eating a healthy diet either." Dr. Ralph assumed as Avery weakly smiled and dabbed.

"Ok, sometimes we can go through trauma, like death or divorce and the stress of single parenthood, and arguments, and we do fine like you did. You are a strong girl and smart too, but after awhile, it all sinks in and one more thing can throw us over the edge, like the way your relationship ended with this new man. Your diet has a lot to do with how you feel also. Avery, you are suffering with a bout of depression."

"Does that mean I am mentally ill? Will I ever be able to get over this?" Avery knew she was depressed but hearing her doctor say it was a little frightening.

"Let's just say you are depressed, and yes, this will go away. Dr. Ralph began writing on his small prescription pad. I am going to prescribe some anti-depressants for you. Now, your diet is very important in the treatment of depression, I want you to start eating at least three balanced meals a day. Eat plenty of fruits and vegetables. No skipping meals or fast foods."

"Actually, Dr. Ralph, I feel a little silly having told you my whole life's story, but I feel a little better already. Thank you for listening, you're great at it."

"Just don't tell my wife, she tells me I haven't heard a word she has said for forty years." Dr. Ralph handed Avery the prescription and patted her on the shoulder as they walked out of the room together.

During the next few weeks, she would think she was feeling a little better; then she would hear a message from Grant. He sounded so sweet, so sincere. Instead of an uncontrollable sadness she was able to become angry. *Why in the hell had he succumbed to Tara? Wasn't sex with her good enough that she should have made him forget about Tara.* In her mind she knew that it wasn't really about sex, it was about loving someone and not being able to control yourself even if you knew it was bad for you and that was exactly why she couldn't and wouldn't talk to Grant. She refused to put herself in the position he had obviously put himself into, loving Tara and trying to fool himself and the rest of the world into believing that he was in love with her.

After a while Grant quit leaving any messages at all. He quit trying. Avery didn't blame him. But at the same time she missed hearing his voice on her machine. Maybe it would be easier to get over him if she didn't hear his voice.

One evening after the children were asleep, Avery decided she was strong enough to check her e-mail. She felt the need to read what Grant wrote even though she dreaded to re-live that night. For some reason, she thought maybe if she read it that it would help her to close the door once and for all on her feelings for Grant and the relationship she thought they had. She was starting to realize one thing, and it might have been a little odd, but she had learned from Grant how to really love someone, and what qualities were important to look for in a man.

She even found herself thinking that she was glad even for the short time they had spent together because she knew that some people go through their whole life and don't find what she had with Grant. She and Grant had been wonderful together, like a fairy tail or romance novel; if only it had been real.

She opened her mail from Grant. It was dated over a month ago. *Avery, please, please read this.*

Tears ran down her cheeks as she read Grant's explanation of the fateful evening. How she wished she could believe him. She knew better than to even think about believing something so absurd. Had not she learned from Peter the lengths men would go to cover up an indiscretion? Besides, he had not tried to call her in weeks. *I imagine he has totally forgotten me. He must be dating someone else by now. Lisa told me that Tara is still dating Ragon. She just uses Grant. What kind of hold could she possibly have on him? What a shame!* Avery deleted the mail and went to bed.

During the days she busied herself with tennis and activities for the boys, but at night, every single night, after she put the boys to bed, she prayed for Grant and his happiness. She couldn't keep her loneliness at bay. It would come flooding back to her and grab at her chest like the fear of a bad dream that reoccurs over and over again. You know it is going to come but you can't possibly stop it, you can only dread the inevitability of it.

School was out for the summer. Peter and Avery had finally been able to work out a schedule for summer visitation after weeks of arguments. Peter wanted to take the children and keep them from Avery's "bad influence" by putting them in day care at their school. Avery didn't want the boys to have to be with a sitter or in daycare if they could be doing fun things with her during the day. Peter finally agreed to let Avery see the boys on some days during his visitation periods if she would agree to give him his full abatement. They would take turns with the children every two weeks for summer visitation. Peter was starting to be a little more civil lately, since she wasn't dating anyone. When Peter came to pick up the boys Wednesday evening he had told her, with a sexy smile, that anytime she felt like she needed to *be with* someone, she could feel free to come over to his house. *That cheating jerk! I wonder what his little girlfriend would think if she thought Peter had propositioned her. It would serve her right to know that she had such a loyal boyfriend! I would rather die than to succumb to Peter's cheating conquests! How in the world can Peter ever trust her or how can she ever trust him? What makes either of them think that if they cheated on their husband and wife that they will be faithful to each other? What kind of a relationship can you have without trust? Just why in the hell couldn't Grant have felt that way!* And then, the sadness would engulf her at the thought of Tara and Grant and she would have to shake it off and busy herself with thoughts of other things.

Her mother told her that when she felt depressed to do something nice for someone else. That actually seemed to help, along with the drugs. Avery decided that as soon as the boys went back to school this fall, she would get a job. She had to do something different in her life. She had to find something to make her forget.

Peter still seemed to know what Avery did and where she went at all times. He was probably having her followed to try to get something on her. He still couldn't take the blame for their failed marriage. Avery could care less. It didn't bother her much more than an insect flying around her face would.

She just hated that he was wasting the boy's inheritance, and told him so when he slipped and told her he "knew where she was or what she did."

"Avery, call your mother." The message machine told her as she walked into her back door facing a sink full of dirty dishes.

"Hey, Mom, I just got in from taking the boys to the club for a tennis lesson. This is their first day, you know. They will be taking a lesson every Wednesday morning for six weeks, except the week we go to Florida."

"Are they excited about going to Florida?"

"Yes, they can't wait. They have told all of their friends about their yearly Me Me vacation."

"Well, I can't wait either. Piper has made reservations at a condo right on the beach with a pool, tennis courts, and it's a two bedroom."

"Thank goodness! We are still going to be cramped for space. Does she have the sleeping arrangements worked out?"

"Yep, she has you sleeping with me on a double bed in one bedroom, Liza and Piper in twin beds in the other bedroom.."

Avery interrupted, "Oh, fine, I get to sleep with the one who snores!"

"Yep, that's the price you pay for not living here and being able to put your dibs in first! Of course, I will be happy to have the bed myself if you would rather sleep on the floor in the living room with the kids, ha!."

"I'll just bring a good pair of ear plugs." Avery teased her mother.

"Anyway, they have Nick and Leigh on the pull down cots in a hallway and the rest of the kids on the floor in the living room on sleeping bags. There will be all eleven of us this year."

"Nick is going?"

"Yes, can you believe it? He said he wouldn't want to miss this MeMe vacation for the world; too many opportunities to see hot babes in their bikinis."

"I am so glad. We will have so much fun. I am really looking forward to it, Mom."

"Good, you be here next Sunday night around 6:00. We decided to drive at night so the little ones can sleep and then we will be there in time to check in on Monday morning. Nick can help us drive."

"Great, Mom. Well be there."

"OK, baby, I'll see you Sunday."

"Bye, Mom, I love you."

Jimmie didn't ask Avery if she had talked to Grant, she knew better. This time it was going to take more than a few weeks or months to heal her broken heart.

Avery hung up the phone from her mother with her spirits a little higher than they had been in weeks. Nick was going on the MeMe vacation with them this year. Last year he had not gone because he thought he was way too mature at sixteen. This year, maybe he realized that his aunts and grandmother were quite a fun group to be with even though he had to put up with all of the younger cousins, brother and sister, Leigh.

Nick was Liza's first child, the first grandchild, and Avery and Piper's first nephew. The girls adored their nephew and he adored his aunts. He was born when Avery was starting high school and Piper was in Junior high. Liza, Calvin, Liza's husband, and two year old Nick moved into the Lynch home with Jimmie and Bill for a year when Nick was only two years old. Calvin had lost his job so Bill and Jimmie invited them to stay with them until Calvin found a job. Then, after Calvin got a job, they stayed for another several months to save money while their new house was being built.

I t was during this time that the bond between Avery and Nick was formed. After school, she took him everywhere she went; to the mall, to friend's homes, even on some dates. Avery and Piper would teach him to sing all of the popular songs like "Little Red Corvette" by Prince and "Mercedes" by Paula Abdul. They had stayed close to him from the time he was a loveable tot, doing anything to please his aunts until now. He had grown up from a chunky, precocious little boy to a gorgeous hunk of an almost man.

He stood over six feet two inches with blonde hair and the same golden skin of Avery. His eyes were the clearest of blues where hers were brown. He was a clean cut, well dressed teen with a good heart, his stubborn and independent ways had gotten him into trouble on more than one occasion but his charm and good looks had kept him in favor with teachers and friends alike. He was a golden boy.

Like Avery, he was very popular with his peers and the girls chased him mercilessly. If he found a girl he may want to date and she started calling him, he would loose interest immediately. He needed a challenge. Occasionally, when Avery came home for a weekend, she would leave her boys with their grandparents and take Nick out on the town. They both knew they were very much alike. There was nothing he felt he couldn't talk to Avery about from his football games, girlfriends, parties, and even about the drugs he had tried or was tempted to try. Avery never acted shocked or lectured him like his mother did. She always seemed to understand and then would tell him tales of what happened to some of her friends in college who drank too much or took drugs.

Nick appreciated her style even though he was smart enough to know that the stories were her way of trying to talk him out of doing something that was probably stupid.

Avery had been there for him when his parents divorced when he was thirteen. It was a shocking blow to him and he had angry, bitter feelings for both his mother and father for tearing up the family. It was Avery who listened to him and took him riding around in the car for hours just so he could talk and get away from his troubles. She had always been careful not to bad mouth his father for cheating on his mother even though she had to bite her tongue several times not to. Now he felt it was his turn to be there for Avery. That is why he decided to go on the MeMe vacation this year even though he would have to put up with all of the screaming little cousins, Jason, Hunter, Savannah, Marky and Nick's brother Gage and Leigh.

Destin Florida wouldn't be too bad. It might even be a pretty good place for his raging hormones to be the June before his senior year. He had seen movies about kids and their parties on "Spring Break" in Destin and he didn't mind looking for love in all the wrong places even if he didn't find it.

Grant was miserable. He tried and tried to talk to Avery but she would not answer her phone or return his calls. He didn't blame her. He knew what she was thinking and the scene she had walked in on could not have looked any worse. He didn't even know if anyone else would believe the truth if he told him or her really happened. It would sound pretty far- fetched. He felt totally helpless. Tara was truly the devil. He decided that Avery deserved better and there was nothing he could do if she refused to talk to him so he buried himself into his work again.

The office staff knew something was wrong with Dr. Jones. He was still very caring and methodical with his patients but between patients he was quiet. Not at all the happy man they had gotten used to in the last few months. He didn't smile much anymore and his serious demeanor put the nurses on edge. He quit going out for lunch and stayed in the office working on patient files. He quit taking days off and stayed late in the evenings going over lab reports again and again. Several times one of the nurses would quietly try to get his attention "Dr. Jones, Dr. Jones", but if he ignored them they would leave the room and go away. He couldn't seem to concentrate and he wanted to make sure that he wasn't missing anything when his patient's lives were at steak.

One day when he was deep into one of his patient's files he over heard two of the staff nurses talking about some man who was in a coma, "Well," one said to the other, "he slipped into a coma a couple of days ago and we can't seem to rouse him. I'm afraid he won't last much longer. You had better call the family in." Grant made a mental note to ask the nurse who they were talking about later. He didn't know of any of his patients in a coma, must be one of Jim's patients. When he did leave to go home, he sometimes would stop by the bookstore and listen to some new music C.Ds, but his thoughts were of Avery and his depression and hopelessness grew worse. *I guess Avery has completely put me out of her mind. I would leave her alone for the rest of my life if only I could be with her one more time and explain to her what really happened. I love her so much; I don't want her to think that all men will treat her like Peter did and like she thought I did. She is such a beautiful person. I don't want her to live the rest of her life alone, even if I am not the one to be with her. I hope I'm not around to see her with anyone else. I don't think I could stand that. I certainly don't want to be anywhere around Tara, I wish I could move as far away as possible from her! Damn it, that's it! I am going to put the house on the market and move. She will have to drive way the hell out of her way to sneak up or spy on me again!*

As Grant was listening to a new country release by Clint Black one evening at the book store, he thought he heard his youngest son call his name again. He took the headset off of his head and looked around the empty store to see if he could see him. When he was satisfied that his son was not in the store, he put the headset back on and wondered why he was imagining that he was hearing his youngest son call his name. This was not the first time it had happened. He decided that it must be the guilt he felt for leaving the boys with their mother instead of trying to get custody of them.

He dismissed the thought with a wave of his hand and began making mental plans to put the house on the market and move out of the neighborhood as far from Tara as he could get.

He went home and put in a call to Lisa, Avery's friend the real estate agent.

"Lisa, this is Grant Jones, do you remember me?"

"Why, yes, I do Dr. Jones."

"Please call me Grant. I am thinking about selling my house and Avery said that you were the best."

"Well, I'll have to thank Avery for the compliment."

"Have you talked to Avery lately?"

"Yes, as a matter of fact I have. She is planning a trip with her family to Destin Florida this month."

"That's nice, that must be the Me Me vacation she told me about. Say, do you think you could come over here to see the house tomorrow evening around eight?"

"Sure, are you really ready to move?"

"Yes, I need a change." Lisa could tell from Grant's voice that he was mentally down.

"Grant, where do you think you may want to relocate?"

"Maybe out west of town, I don't know for sure. I'll try to sell the house and then decide."

"That is probably a good idea. I'll be there around eight o'clock tomorrow night. Will you be ready for me to put the sign in the yard then?"

"Yes, go ahead. The address is 2912 Country Club Lane. By the way, if you talk to Avery, will you tell her hello for me?"

"Sure, I will be happy to. I was sorry to hear that you guys weren't dating anymore."

"Yes, me too. I guess I will see you tomorrow night."

Grant hung up the phone. He loved his home but it wasn't worth the emotional cost of living so close to Tara.

Grant had only met Lisa once, the first time he had gone out with Avery on the blind date, but he chose to call Lisa because he knew that she was a member of the professional organization, NAR, and knew she had an edge on the marketing of real estate. He also secretly hoped Lisa would give him tidbits about Avery and his heart quickened at the prospect of getting to hear anything about her, although he wasn't ready to offer any information about his love life with a near stranger.

Avery and the boys pulled into the Lynch driveway around 6:00 P.M. to find luggage, bags and pillows piled on the front porch waiting to be loaded into Avery's car. Her spirits were high for the first time in weeks and she was ready for an escape to some lazy days on the beach with the surf and sun and her family.

Florida was all she had hoped it would be; crowded condo with excited children, hours lounging on the beach with her family, cards, and games with the children, and great seafood in the evenings.

Avery, Liza, Piper and Nick went to several local clubs after the little ones were in bed at the condo with their grandmother. They sipped on tropical drinks while watching the locals and tourists twirl, bump, and grind on the dance floors. On several occasions a local drunk or well- meaning man would try to get one of the girls to dance, but none wanted the attention and resented the intrusion into their private party.

One evening after returning to the condo Nick and Avery walked along the beach together. The moon was a distant white disk, low in the sky shining soft beams of light that were magnified on the waves of the lapping waters. Avery held her sandals in one hand and walked next to the water so the tide could barely reach her feet. Nick asked Avery why she was so quiet.

"Oh, Nick, I have just had a lot on my mind."

"Yeah, well you don't fool me, like you are depressed or something."

"Just promise me that you won't get married until you are certain that the girl you want to marry is the girl you will be faithful to all of your life."

"Hey! I'm never getting married!"

"You say that now, but someone will come along that will make you change your mind. I just hope it isn't until you have finished college."

"You don't have to worry about that!"

Avery couldn't help but wonder if Grant ever thought of her anymore. She couldn't seem to get him out of her mind.

"Grant and I walked on the beach in Miami just like this one night."

"You were really in love with him, huh, Ave?"

"Yes, I was. You know, I didn't really know what love was until I met Grant, so I owe him a lot for teaching me what real love is suppose to feel like. Oh, I had fun with Peter and I thought I loved him, but I didn't really. I just didn't realize it, I didn't know any better."

"Why don't you call Grant?"

"It's not that simple, Nick. You see he probably felt about me like I felt about Peter. Grant and I really had fun together and I don't think he realized that he still loved his first wife for awhile."

"How could he love a wench like that?" From what you said she treated him like a dumb ass."

"I don't know. He is too good for his own good, maybe."

"Shit, Avery, you are still in love with the guy, aren't you?"

"I guess so. I can't seem to quit thinking about him but I'm sure he doesn't think about me. He quit calling after a couple of weeks. You know, a one sided love won't work. I'll get over it."

"I'd quit calling after a few days! But if it makes you feel any better, all of my friends think you are one hot chick!"

"Gee, thanks Nick." Avery laughed, "I'll race you back to the condo!"

"Hurry up boys, get up! Your tennis lesson is today! Avery shook the sleepy boys awake. They were still tired from the week of constant going with their cousins in Florida. They had only been home for two days and they did not want to go anywhere today! Avery and the boys pulled up to the courts and the little boys ran into the pro shop to sign in while Avery stopped to chat with Mary Beth in the parking lot.

"Hunter! Jason! I didn't know you guys were taking tennis lessons. How have you guys been doing?"

The boys turned to see Grant standing in the pro shop. Jason ran and threw his arms around Grants legs to give him a tight hug. Hunter stood back and looked at Grant with big sad eyes, it was if he was afraid of Grant.

"How have you guys been, Hunter?"

"We've been fine, sir, we just got back from Florida." Hunter answered him.

"Wow! I bet that was fun!" Grant animated his comments for the boys.

"Yeah, and they buwied me in the sand! Jason looked up at Grant from the bear hold he still had on his legs, pouting his disapproval of being mistreated. Grant rubbed Jason's back and laughed.

"How come you haven't come to see us in a vewy long time, Mistoe Gwant?"

"Hunter could not stand the pretence any longer. He started with an angry accusation. "How come you made my mommy cry?"

Grant knelt down to get on the same level as the little boys. "I didn't mean to make your mommy cry. I am so sorry she was sad. Is she alright now?"

"I guess." Hunter was very standoffish to Grant.

"Hunter, I am so glad to see you guys. Thank you for telling me that your mommy has been sad. I'm going to try to see to it that she will not be sad ever again. I love your mother like you do, and I want her to be happy too. Will you guys help me to try to make her happy again?"

Hunter and Jason just looked at Grant with puzzled looks on their faces.

"Listen, all you guys have to do is don't tell her that I am here and I'll work on a plan. I want very much to come to your house and see you very soon, do you think you can do that Jason?"

"Yea! Will you bwing me a pwize?" Jason was jumping up and down with excitement.

"You know it! Hunter, is that ok with you?"

"I guess so."

"Great! Now, you guys better get out to the courts, Travis and Trent are already out there."

Grant watched Avery talking to Mary Beth through the window of the pro shop. He loved watching her animated personality. He noticed how tan and beautiful her skin was and how the blonde highlights in her hair shimmered in the morning sun. She looked a little thinner, but so gorgeous. He longed to run to her, to hold her and to love her.

Someday, he would prove his love for her. Someday soon she would know the truth. Until then, he knew it would be a lost cause to try to see or talk to her. When she came into the pro shop, Grant slipped upstairs and watched the boys play tennis from the upstairs deck and every once in a while, he caught a glimpse of Avery walking in and out of the pro shop between sets and his heart would ache.

Thursday morning Julie Kramer called just after Avery had crawled out of bed. "Hey, Avery, does Peter have the kids this weekend, specifically Saturday night?"

"Yes, he does, Avery sleepily answered.

"How come, did you need me to baby-sit? I can, It doesn't matter to me if the boys are here or not."

"No, I need you to go out with us this weekend. Jim and I have to take this guy out to dinner. Jim is thinking about hiring him in Grant's place."

"What do you mean in Grant's place?"

"Oh, didn't you know? Grant is leaving the clinic and moving out of town."

"No, I haven't heard that. I don't blame him, he needs to get away form his ex-wife. Maybe he can forget her and get on with his life if he moves away."

"Well, back to me. I don't want to sit at the restaurant like a bump on a log while Jim and this guy are talking business, so would you please go to dinner with us; with me?"

"Julie, this is not a ploy to fix me up with this guy, is it? I am not going out again with any man for years, if ever!"

"No, honestly, I just need someone to talk to while they talk business, in fact, I think he is married or dating someone or something."

"Well, in that case, I don't have anything else to do so it sounds wonderful. Sorry, I sounded sort of glum, about not having anything else to do. I really didn't mean it like it sounded. I guess you heard that I am not seeing Grant anymore."

"I did hear that in fact from Jim and from some of the nurses. They say he is really miserable about it."

"Julie, I walked in on him and Tara having sex. I don't know what he had to be down about unless she has dumped him again."

"Avery, you are wrong about his feelings for Tara, I can assure you that he has no love for her."

"I guess men are all alike. Peter said that about his girlfriend. Not love; just sex! Well screw me running! Sorry, Julie, I am a little bitter right now."

"Hey, it's alright. I would be furious! Have you talked to him since that ordeal?"

"No, what's the use. He has even quit trying to get in touch with me. He isn't totally ignorant; he was there and knows what I saw. I doubt he cares what I think anyway. How could he? He knew I was coming to his house that morning."

"I think he cares much more than you could know. But I completely understand how you must feel. Ok, back to me, again! I am glad you are coming. Jim and I will pick you up at seven. Look stunning as you usually do; we are going to the restaurant at the club and Ave, thanks for going; you will save me from a dreadfully boring evening and you can tell me all of the gory details then, ok?"

"I'll make a deal with you; we won't talk about Grant and I will be the life of the party."

"Ok, I won't say a word, and you are always the life of the party anyway."

"Thanks, Julie. Thank you for inviting me, it really will be nice to get out."

"See you then at seven."

Saturday night came quickly. Avery had not had a chance to shop for anything to wear. Most of her summer clothes were casual so Saturday afternoon she stopped by Janie's, at Janie's own suggestion, and borrowed a fitted, greenish gold file cocktail dress, sleeveless, with very wide shoulder straps, kind of a 1950s revival of a sleeveless shift. Naturally, Janie had shoes, bag, and jewelry to match. Janie seemed happy that Avery was going out tonight. She normally would be feeling a little left out if she herself had nothing to do, and Avery would feel the guilt for going without her. Tonight seemed different to Avery. Janie was practically dressing her and throwing her out to dinner at the club with excitement. *They better not be trying to fix me up with this guy.* That thought crossed her mind more than once.

Jim and Julie arrived at Avery's house promptly at seven. Jim got out of the car to go to the door and Avery came outside just as he closed the car door.

"I wish my wife were as prompt!" Jim said to Avery teasing his wife.

"I've had two days to get ready for this with no children." Avery laughed and winked at Julie in the front seat of the black Lincoln as she scooted onto the gray leather back seat while Jim held open the door for her. Avery loved the "new car smell" of leather seats.

"What a darling dress!" Julie said admiring Janie's outfit. "I told you to look stunning, I didn't say to look like a damn model!"

"Ha! Julie, you are way too kind. This is Janie's dress, thank goodness; I have lost a little weight and luckily could fit into it."

The car sped off to the club as the girls chatted.

Jim dropped the girls off at the Massive wooden front doors of the Baton Rouge Country Club and he drove off to park the car. The summer evening was warm and humid but the girls waited outside for Jim to come join them.

Jim held open one of the mammoth doors with huge circles of brass hinged to the doors as doorknockers. They entered the foyer and stepped into the bar room where the dim lights made it possible to see only the light reflecting off of the glasses hanging over the heavy oak bar that stretched across one wall of the room.

The smell of liquor was heavy in the air. Jim ordered the girls and himself a cocktail while they stood at the bar waiting on a table.

Soon after the bartender handed them their drinks, Jim spotted a table in the center of the room with four chairs and led the women to the coveted seats.

"Dale is supposed to meet us here in the bar. Be looking for a tall, thin, young guy with red hair, girls"

Julie and Avery sipped their drinks and chatted with Jim as they watched for Dale at the door.

Avery noticed her friend Lisa walking in with two other woman. "Look, Julie, there is Lisa. I am so glad she is getting out."

"Yea, me too. I bet she misses Bob terribly!"

"She does. He was her best friend. It must be horrible for her. I thought she came in with some other girls, but I only see Lisa now."

Julie began waving her arm high above her head to get Lisa's attention.

Lisa spotted them in the dim light and rushed over to greet her friends.

"Avery, Julie, I am so glad to see you guys." Lisa looked beautiful. The smart black dress made her dark eyes sparkle.

"Hey, Avery, what have you been doing? I've missed seeing you at the bagel hut, you world traveler!"

"Yeah, fun in the sun and all of that!"

"Julie, when the kids were in school, I would meet Janie and Lisa at the Bagel Hut a couple of mornings a week. It was not planned, but really fun. Occasionally, we would run into Amy, one of Lisa's friends who happens to be Tara's best friend and get some scoop on Tara. Next year you will have to come have breakfast with us some mornings."

"Sounds great; I'll do that maybe." Julie said, not meaning a word of it.

"Lisa, have you run into Amy there lately?"

Lisa didn't have time to answer Avery's question, Julie interrupted, "Lisa, is it all set?"

"Yes."

About then Jim spotted Dale walking into the bar and excused himself to greet the newcomer.

"Is what all set?" Avery asked Julie, looking puzzled.

Lisa responded to her question.

"Avery, you know that we are some of your best friends."

"Of course I do."

"You know that we would never do anything to hurt you, don't you?"

"Yes." Avery was getting a little wary of this line of questioning.

Lisa continued as if Avery was in the third grade again and Lisa was the teacher, breaking bad news to her as gently as possible. "We have a surprise for you that you will not like at first, but we know you will love it later."

"Lisa, what in the world are you talking about?"

"Come in the ladies room and we will tell you."

Julie scooted her chair back on the dense carpet as she stood up. Avery sat looking up at Julie like she was apprehensive of getting out of her chair.

"Come on, silly, it's not that big of a deal." Julie prodded her to get up.

"Ok, you know, my birthday is not until November."

"Oh, really. Darn the luck. Why did we think it was today?" Lisa teased.

The three girls walked across the bar to the ladies room and walked into the massive lounge brightly decorated with yellow wallpaper splashed with enormous cream and red poppies. A huge Japanese vase full of silk flowers matching the wallpaper sat on a low glass table in the center of a seating area at one end of the lounge. At the opposite end of the lounge, hung gilded mirrors on the wall over marble hand sinks and stacks of white linen hand towels.

The girls led Avery over to one of the soft, rose-colored couches encircling the glass table. They made themselves comfortable, Lisa pulled a pack of cigarettes from her purse and offered Avery and Julie one. Avery took one and Lisa lit her cigarette after she lit her own. Avery was taking a deep drag on her cigarette when she noticed the figure of a trim lady standing in the doorway between the lounge and the bathroom. She adjusted her eyes and blinked. She immediately got sick at her stomach and started to get up to leave.

Lisa grabbed Avery's arm and stopped her.

"Avery, Tara and our mutual friend, Amy came with me tonight. Tara wants to talk to you. She has something very important to tell you."

Avery looked at Lisa with anger boiling in her eyes.

"Avery, please. Just listen to what Tara has to say; then we will leave." Julie tried to soothe Avery.

Lisa invited Tara and Amy into the lounge to join them on the couches.

Tara walked over to stand by the glass table where she could look down on the three girls sitting on the couch. Amy appeared in the same doorway and leaned on the doorframe. Tara started to speak and then she hesitated. The three girls were looking up at her in anticipation. She began again slowly. "Avery, I want to tell you that I am very sorry for what happened at Grant's house. He didn't tell me he was expecting you."

"I'm sure he didn't care if I was coming or not, if you were there." Avery frowned waving the obnoxious smoke from her face trying to be civil to Tara.

"No, it wasn't what you thought. I was angry with Grant and I know this sounds silly, but have you ever seen a picture in the society section of the newspaper of one of your old boyfriends announcing the approaching marriage of he and some other woman, and for some reason you felt betrayed, like he was suppose to love only you forever? It didn't matter that you had not thought of him in years or that you didn't even really even like him that much. It was just a pride thing. Has anyone else ever felt that?"

The three girls looked at each other. Lisa and Julie gave a shrug; Avery just sat on the couch and took another puff of her cigarette.

Tara looked directly at Avery. "Well, I was furious at Grant for leaving town and not telling me how to reach him in case I had an emergency with one of the boys and I had also heard that you and Grant were talking about getting married. I guess I just thought he would never marry again and I wanted to see if I had any influence over him anymore.

Avery slouched down in the couch staring at Tara in disbelief. "Tara, you are already married. How do you think your husband would feel about this?"

"Look Avery, at the time I didn't think about that. Do you want to hear this or not?" Avery had no expression, she just looked at Tara.

"Please go on and tell her Tara", Lisa pleaded.

After a long hesitation, Tara began to speak in a matter of fact : "I had a key to the house. I let myself in and was wearing only a trench coat. When Grant heard the door open, he said something like fix you a cup of coffee and he would be right in, so I took my coat off and was going to try to seduce him.

When he came in the kitchen he was wearing only a towel and when he saw me, he became furious."

Avery sat stiffly with her mouth drawn tightly, taking in every word.

"He started yelling at me to give him the key to his house. That only made me madder. I grabbed him and kissed him hard to be mean and he kept trying to pull me off of him. We wrestled like that for a while and that's when his towel fell off. I hung onto him and we fell over onto the couch. That is when you came in. "Avery, I am sorry. I am really not a mean person. I don't know what got into me. All I know is that Gant is really in love with you and our marriage and any feelings he has had for me or any I have had for him disappeared long ago. I hope we can be friends, Avery. I didn't mean to hurt you. I just wanted to get back at Grant."

Avery sat silent on the couch, stunned.

"Anyway, I wanted to tell you the truth. Let's go Amy."

Avery finally found her voice. "Wait Tara," Avery hesitated as if she were trying to find the words. "Thank you for telling me this. I would never have believed anyone else."

"Yea, I kind of thought that."

Tara still stood facing Avery sitting on the couch with her hands clasp tightly on her lap.

"Tara, I don't know if I will see Grant again or not, but if I do, you will always have my respect for telling me this. And, I promise, if we do get back together, I will never say anything negative about you to your sons. They are precious boys and you are doing a great job with them. I hope we can be friends."

"Thanks, Avery. Maybe we can but I doubt it because of Grant. While I am telling it all… you should know that he is a control freak and very irresponsible. But, better you than me.

Lisa, are you and Amy ready to go?"

Lisa got off of the couch and hugged Avery then she walked out of the lounge with Tara and Amy. Avery stood watching them leave. *Grant had been telling the truth! Oh, my God. What have I done?*

Julie broke the silence. "Hey, let's go call Grant on his cell phone."

"Julie, I couldn't. He must hate me. I have been so stubborn. I never even gave him a chance to explain what happened. He may be dating someone else by now." Avery paced as she talked to Julie. Julie put her hand on Avery's arm to still her. "Ave, look at me. Why do you think we got this all orchestrated? Grant loves you. He is miserable. That is why he is moving."

"Oh, my God, he is moving!"

"Uh, yeah! Here is my phone. Call him, or have you forgotten his number?"

Avery stared at the phone. She hesitated and then she grabbed the phone and dialed his number.

"Grant?"

"Avery, how are you?"

"Grant, I just called to tell you how very sorry I am."

"What do you have to be sorry for, princess?" Tears started to well up in Avery's eyes at hearing his voice.

"For not letting you explain what happened. I just ran into Tara and she told me the whole story."

"I am the one who is sorry, Avery. I never meant to hurt you."

"I know that now, and I am so sorry that I hurt you by not letting you tell me what happened. Grant, I am feeling very sick. Do you think I could make a house call to your place tonight?"

"I would love nothing better."

Julie tugged on Avery's arm. Avery turned to see Julie motion that she was going out to join the men. Avery nodded in understanding.

"I am at the club with Jim and Julie while he interviews a new guy to take your place. What is this about you moving?'

"I'll save that for tonight. You better go join them and I will be dreaming about you until you get here."

"Ok, Grant, thank you for forgiving me."

"There was nothing to forgive. I love you, Avery."

Avery hung up the phone and walked over to the hand basin to dab her eyes with one of the linen hand towels. She straightened her hair and her dress and put on another coat of lipstick then surveyed herself in the mirror. *Gee, I'm glad Janie had this cute little number for me to wear now!* She smiled at the thought of seeing Grant tonight and hoped she could contain herself during dinner. She would call Lisa in the morning and find out how she and Amy coordinated all of this. Avery then walked over and opened the massive door of the lounge to enter the bar when she noticed a man standing in the hallway as if waiting for her. She looked more closely and realized it was Grant! Grant was holding a single, long stemmed, red rose bud. He walked over to meet her and handed the rose to her while he gently took her arm with his other hand and bend down to kiss her cheek.

"I love you," he whispered. He then put his arm around her waist and escorted her to the table where their party was waiting. All through dinner and the business meeting neither could keep their eyes off of each other. They waited until the meeting and dinner was over before they excused themselves and left together.

Part 11

Grant put his silver gray Durango in drive and took Avery's hand while he maneuvered the turn out onto the street from the club parking lot with one hand. They drove in near silence to his house, looking at each other and smiling. As they pulled into the driveway of Grant's house, he looked at her and said. "We've got a lot of catching up to do. I hope you didn't have to get home in

a hurry. I didn't even think to ask you if you had to get home to the boys."

"I would have told you when we left if I did; they are at their dad's this week. We can catch up all night." Avery grinned sheepishly at Grant.

Grant pulled the car into the garage and pushed the button to the garage door to close. Once inside he poured each of them a glass of Chablis and they curled up on his couch together. Soft music was already playing in the background and a single lamp was glowing in the window.

"Ok, now, how did you arrange all of this?" Avery sat up with a serious look wanting to know all of the details.

"Well, I listed the house with Lisa and as we got to know each other better our conversations always seemed to end up centered around you. She knew how miserable I was without you and it seems that Tara was getting all of her information about us from her friend, Amy, who was getting it from Lisa. She started out by trying to get me to call you, but I knew it wouldn't do a bit of good unless you heard the truth from Tara, herself. Once we put two and two together, Lisa thought up the plan. The tricky part was getting you to go with Julie to the club tonight. Lisa said you refused to go out with anyone wearing pants."

"I really let my insecurities get in the way of any sense of reason, didn't I?"

"Avery, that is all in the past. All I want to do now is to love you and for us to be together as much a humanly possible. In fact, I want you to go away with me for a few days to Aruba next week. And, I am really glad you didn't want to go out with anyone else wearing pants." Grant leaned over and kissed her sweetly.

"Will the boys still be with Peter? I know its short notice, but I really want you to go."

"Oh, Grant, I would love to! I've never been to Aruba. The boys will still be staying with Peter then. How exciting, I've always wanted to go to Aruba!"

"Don't get too excited, it's for another medical conference. I was dreading it until now." Grant smiled at Avery and kissed her again on her neck. "You know, Avery, I have insecurities too. It is hard not to when you have been fooled so completely in the past by someone you trusted, like we both have. I am just so very sorry that you were hurt."

"Grant, I don't ever want you to feel insecure about my feelings for you. I know more than ever that you are the love of my life. The only man I have ever truly loved, and even though I was so crushed at what I thought was going on between you and Tara, I was glad that I had been lucky enough to have had the kind of relationship with you that we had."

"You mean have, and will always have. Nothing is ever going to pull us apart again, deal?"

"Deal! Now, what is this about you moving?"

"Avery, I need to get away from Tara even if it is just across town. I don't know, I don't want to get too far from the boys, but I need to get away from her, out of this neighborhood."

"What about the guy you and Jim were talking to tonight. Isn't he going to take your place?"

"We need another doctor to take some of the load off of us whether I leave the practice or not. I just don't know yet what I am going to do. You will be the first to know, I promise." Grant took Avery in his arms and kissed her soft lips and her neck as he whispered, "It is so good to have you home."

They kissed deeply and passionately. Avery felt tears rush to her eyes. They both felt the love well up in their hearts and knew the respect, friendship, and love they had for each other could never be destroyed.

The 747 landed in Aruba around 5:30 P.M. on Friday. The flight over had been relatively smooth. Avery and Grant tried to learn a few phrases of the Papiamento language on the flight over. They giggled as they tried to speak to each other. "Mi stima aworo!" Avery whispered sexily in Grant's ear.

"I think you just said, I love later." Grant said chuckling.

"Ha! But I do, yeah, that is what I meant to say, I love later, and you better be ready too!" Avery giggled at herself.

"Well, Mi stima bai, I think." Grant whispered sexily in Avery's ear.

"You think! You rat! Well, I love you to, I think!" Avery teased Grant nudging him with her shoulder.

After they found their bags on the conveyor belt in the Queen Beatrix terminal they walked outside to hail a cab. A warm breeze rushed over them and they could see white, powdery sand for miles. Avery remarked that the short trees dotting the white sands of the desert island were all leaning inward, away from the clear blue waters of the sea.

"Those trees are called Divi Divi trees. They all grow that way."

Avery admired Grant's intelligence. She knew of his reputation as a very knowledgeable and wonderful heart surgeon but even the smallest of things like his knowing what Divi Divi trees were made her terribly proud that Grant was the man she was in love with.

Aruba was a fabulous, beautiful island. An exotic panorama of white desert sands coupled with the shimmering turquoise waters of the Caribbean Sea.

A yellow and black taxi pulled up to the waiting couple immediately. The driver threw the gearshift in park, popped the trunk latch and quickly ran around the back of the cab to load the bags into his trunk. He was a small, dark man with a mustache and an expressionless face.

"Wyndham Aruba, please." Grant gave instructions to the taxi driver as they slid into the back seat of the cab.

The taxi driver didn't acknowledge that he heard a thing but mechanically got back into the driver's seat and sped off to parts unknown to Avery and Grant.

The buildings along the picturesque southern coast from a distance looked like a miniature Christmas village set perfectly in order for all to admire in a department store window. The multicolored houses of Wilheminastraat combine carved wood doors and traditional Dutch tiles with open and airy galleries and sloping roofs. Rows of glamorous hotels and casinos lined J. E. Irausquin Boulevard, all with red tile roofs and colorfully painted fronts.

The taxi pulled up to the Casablanca Casino and stopped. The cabbie threw the cab in park, popped the trunk and rushed out to unload the baggage, still expressionless.

"Grant, this is a casino, do you think we are at the wrong place?"

Grant laughed at Avery as he handed the cabbie some bills. This is the Wyndham hotel *and* casino."

"Wow! This is gorgeous! I know what I will be doing while you are in your meetings, CHA-CHING!" Avery acted like she was pulling the handle of a slot machine.

"You can feed those little bandits all you want to, lil darlin," Grant answered in a John Wayne twang.

"Well, I doubt that *any* of you cowboys at this conference can afford my fast arm for three days." Avery laughed. "They don't call me Calamity for nothing!"

After checking in the couple decided to have a relaxing drink on the balcony. They sat content and watched the waves white cap into foamy bubbles onto the clean, white beach. The panoramic view of white sands and brilliantly blue water was spectacular. Grant and Avery dressed for dinner and decided to dine in the lush hotel and then to take an evening walk on the beach they had been admiring.

The restaurant was dripping with glass prism chandeliers hanging low from the ceiling and gold leaf décor. Starched white linen cloths and materdees in black tuxedoes gave the restaurant elegance rather than the usual feel of a casino café. The meal was quite good and the young lovers were anxious to be alone, away from the well-meaning waiters who were a little too anxious to please them.

Tendrils of Avery's blonde hair lifted in the warm breath of the ocean air. The two walked, holding hands along the soft clean sands of Baby's Beach toward the southeastern tip of the island. The beauty of the dazzling waters at dusk presented a stunning spot for a private rendezvous. Tall and slender Grant, with wayward locks of hair, dark silk shirt and gray silk pants billowing in the breeze, holding hands with Avery; her soft crepe skirt blowing between her legs and outlining her slim figure, made them an attractive and coveted silhouette to those watching in the distance. Watchers could see them stop and come together in an embrace to kiss and then to continue their walk.

Once at the tip of the island with twinkling stars above, glittering city lights behind them and sparkling, crystal blue waters as far as they could see around them, they stood, holding each other for what onlookers might have thought a very long time. They became one with nature, with this island, and with each other. Avery could have stayed entwined in Grant's strong arms on that secluded beach forever. Grant took Avery's hands and held them between her breasts and his chest as he looked down into her eyes and said, "Avery, I want you to know something and I want you to humor me and listen very quietly to what I have to say."

"Alright, Grant."

I want you to know that you are all I could ever want. Every time I see you I feel that I am falling in love all over again. I could just stare at your smile and your beauty for hours. I love your sweetness, your kindness and your generosity. I love being with you. I love watching you with our sons, and I love the way you play with them and teach them, and I love having the children with us. Avery, you and the boys make my life complete. You are my home and my room. You are all I need or could ever want. I never want us to be apart again."

"Oh, Grant! How beautiful! Do you really mean all of those things?"

"I mean them from the depths of my soul, I love you, Avery." Grant got down on one knee and looked up at Avery.

She thought she detected his eyes watering as she searched his face in the evening dim.

"Avery, I love you more than I ever thought I could love anyone. I want to spend the rest of my life with you. Will you please marry me?"

Avery dropped to the sand on her knees facing him. "Grant, my love, thank you so much for asking me to marry you. You are the love of my life and I feel that God has put us together. I want to spend the rest of my life with you too. You are my best friend and my soul mate. And I want to marry you with my whole heart, but I am so afraid that you will be taking on more than you realize."

"I am afraid of some things too, Avery, but I think if we truly love each other that we can work through anything."

"Are you sure you are ready to take us on? Would Travis and Trent be OK with having to share you and your home with Jason and Hunter?"

"Avery, they don't live with me and besides, they still would have their own rooms and they would get used to it. I love Jason and Hunter and I know that they will learn to love me too."

"Grant, will you still be fun and romantic and always be my best friend and promise with your life never to cheat on me?"

"You will always be my best friend and you know in your heart that I will never hurt you on purpose."

"Yes, yes, I do know that. That is one of the reasons I love you so much, you are much too kind to ever hurt anyone. Yes! I will marry you, my love." Avery threw her arms around Grants neck and they hugged and kissed and rocked on their knees in the sand until they fell over, laughing in the sand.

Grant and Avery lay on the cool, deserted beach with the surf rolling onto the sand at their feet, gazing up at the millions of stars in the sky.

"Do you care how soon we tie the knot?" Grant asked Avery.

"I will be ready whenever you are."

"I would like our boys to be with us when we do it." Grant spoke seemingly deep in thought.

"That would make it more special. The boys would feel so much more apart of it all if they were with us." Avery agreed. She loved the fact that Grant was so thoughtful of the children.

"I think so too. Let's don't wait too long. I think we need to get started trying to make little Grace." Grant stared up at the stars with a broad grin on his face.

"You are so funny! Do you really want another baby?" Avery was a little surprised that Grant seriously wanted to try to have a child.

"With you I do." Grant pulled Avery close and kissed her. "Yes, I want to have a little girl and I want her to look just like you."

"That is so sweet, Grant. She can look a little like me if she has your smile."

Grant was jolted back to reality, "I almost forgot!" I have something for you." Grant sat up from the sand and got on his knees to dig into his pants pocket. He pulled out a tiny black velvet box and handed it to Avery.

Avery held the tiny box in her hands and looked at Grant. "I don't need one of these to marry you or to love you. I have been married to you in my heart for a very long time." She slowly opened the box and stared for what seemed like an eternity to Grant. Then she said softly and earnestly, "My God, Grant, this is the most beautiful ring I have seen in my entire life. Grant, this ring is fabulous!" She sat staring at the ring with eyes wide. He took the ring out of the box she was holding and slid it on her finger. It twinkled like the stars above them and reflected the lights behind them and it sparkled like the crystal sea around them.

"This ring *is* this night for me. Every time I look at this ring I will remember this night, alone on this beach with you and the beautiful things you said to me. It will always remind me of your love." Avery's tears were those of happiness. "I love you so much, Grant. Thank you. Thank you for this beautiful ring and for loving me enough to ask me to marry you. Thank you for this beautiful evening, but most of all Grant, thank you so much just for being *you*. For being the kind of man you are, truthful, sincere, thoughtful and kind and wonderful and romantic and very handsome and very, very good in… you know!" Avery laughed and grabbed Grant and pulled him down on the sand with her. She kissed him over and over again, "Mi stima Aruba and Mi stima te!"

Grant and Avery consummated their love slowly and sweetly on the deserted beach as the rushing tide kept rythum.

Spent, and happy, they lay in each other's arms looking up at the stars.

Grant was awakened by the sound of a child calling in the distance, "Dad, Dad, can you hear me?"

It bothered him. He sat up and looked around and seeing nothing except darkened beach houses above them, he blew it off and woke Avery for their walk back to the hotel.

CHAPTER 11

Grant and Avery were married on December 30th of that same year. One year and 3 weeks after their fateful blind date. They had a small, family ceremony at the Episcopal Church in Baton Rouge with all four of their children as witnesses. After a small reception given by their parents, Grant and Avery flew off to the beaches of Spain for their honeymoon.

Sitting together on the plane ride home Avery cuddled up to Grant and said, "Grant, I am so ready to start my life as your wife."

Grant looked down at Avery and smiled.

Grant and Avery loaded their bags in the back of the silver Durango they had left at the airport parking lot. Avery was glad to be home and anxious to see the boys. The honeymoon had been wonderful, full of romance and adventure, but for the first time since she and Grant had been seeing each other, she was ready to get back into the "real world" as Mrs. Grant Lee Jones.

"I thought we would drive to St. Charles to see your parents." Grant looked over at Avery as he passed the street to his house.

"Oh, are you sure you want to?" Avery was a little dismayed.

"Yep. I think you will enjoy the visit and we can pick up the boys instead of waiting for the X es bringing them to us."

"Well, OK, I guess that will be fine. I'm sure Mom and Dad will be thrilled, this is so thoughtful of you."

The sun was shining brightly and the crisp January day was perfect for the drive. Grant was a little quiet but Avery had learned that he did need a little down time occasionally so she sat quietly enjoying the scenery that she loved so much. As they came to Stanton Hall, Grant pulled into the driveway and slowly let the car hug the lane where the giant oaks with soft, gray moss suspended from the giant limbs reached out over the lane to caress them with open arms. "Let's take a break here and tour the old place." Grant said as he stopped the car in front of the gigantic front porch. Avery felt a little excitement about getting to see her beloved Stanton Hall.

She never took the time to stop with the boys when she was on her way to visit her parents.

"This is great! You know how I love this old place." She said as Grant came to her side of the car to open the door for her.

They walked up the front steps and onto the front porch hand in hand. Grant opened the massive door and turned to Avery. Grant swooped Avery up in his arms and carried her through the doors into the lovely old foyer.

"Surprise!" Grant let Avery down on the floor as all four of their boys came running into the great hall followed closely behind by Jimmie and Bill Lynch.

"Welcome home, my darling." Grant said to Avery as the mob gathered around them.

"What do you mean welcome home, Grant?"

"Mommie, this is ouw new houth! Gwant bought it fo uth!" Little Jason beamed up at his mother.

Avery turned to Grant with questions in her eyes. "Grant, you can't buy this old home, it is on the Historical Registry. What is he talking about?"

Grant smiled that broad smile of his, "I am talking about this is our new home. Private people can own homes on the National Historic Registry as long as they don't change the historical value of the place. This is my wedding gift to you."

Avery gasped as she threw her arms around Grant's neck to hug him.

"Oh, my God, Grant, I can't believe it! It can't be! Thank you so very much!" She turned to the boys and hugged them all together. "Kids, look! This is a real dream come true, isn't it?"

"Come on Mom, we want to show you around!" Trent and Travis jumped on their dad as Hunter and Jason grabbed their mom's hand to drag her through the house.

"Come on, MeMe!" Hunter cried after Jimmie. Avery called, "Trent, Travis, come show me around."

The excited little boys jumped off of their dad and ran to catch up. Jimmie and the boys went through each room with

Avery while Bill and Grant sat in the parlor with a drink and talked about the trip to Spain.

Avery loved the way Grant's furniture blended with hers in the old home. She still couldn't believe what she was seeing. When they returned to the parlor Avery asked, "Grant, this is too far from the clinic for you to drive everyday. And, you need to be close to the hospitals. What are you going to do?"

"Well, I'm hoping to get some patients to see me at my new heart clinic in St. Charles."

"You're kidding! You really left the clinic?"

"Yes, Oh, I am still affiliated with the heart clinic at Baton Rouge, but I am opening a new branch in St. Charles. You will have to help me with that, you know, public relations, get me some business."

"You know I will!" Avery beamed.

"This is a perfect location. Between your parents, Travis and Trent." Grant mused.

"Hopefully, the boys will move in with us." Avery really thought they might, especially now since they had this wonderful estate to roam around on.

That evening after all of the children were tucked in and Bill and Jimmie had left to go home, Grant took Avery by the hand and they walked hand and hand up the winding staircase to their new bedroom.

As they lay in bed, holding each other Avery said. "Grant, you have made me the happiest woman in the whole world.

If I were to die tonight, I could not have ever wished for anything more. Thank you, my darling. I will always believe that only God could have brought us together"

"Thank you, my love. I feel exactly the same, and I am the luckiest man in the world. Just promise you will always love me."

"Nothing in the world could ever change my mind about my love for you."

"Nor mine for you."

Grant lay next to his new wife in the twilight world between sleep and reality and as he sank deeper into the dream world, he felt his life was complete. Life was good.

Grant looked up to see Avery standing in the doorway. She was radiant in her white chiffon gown and robe. "Avery, what are you doing out of bed? Come to me, darling." She looked so young and beautiful with her hair shining in the moonlight.

"I can't just yet, my love. But, I'll be there soon, very soon." Avery smiled at Grant with all of the love in her heart expressed in her eyes. Oh, Grant, it is so wonderful here: I don't want you to ever be afraid, I won't leave without you. I will be here waiting for you."

"Dad, Dad," Grant heard his youngest son's voice again. Grant's eyes fluttered, then opened. Standing over him was the face of Avery, so beautiful, no, something was a little different. She had tears in her eyes.

"Avery?" Grant was confused. He surveyed his surroundings from his bed. The walls were close; this room was tiny and white. There was one window to his right behind the girl standing by his bedside. There were other people in the room but he couldn't distinguish who they were.

"Daddy, it's me, Grace. Mamma is gone, remember?"

Grace stared into her fathers old, and confused eyes, the once brilliant blue eyes were fogged with cataracts.

Grace turned to the nurse in the hospital room. "He is awake! Get the doctor, please. Daddy, you have been in a coma, can you hear me?"

"Grace?"

"Yes, Daddy, it's Grace. The boys are here too, Daddy." Grant began to realize and remember. "Grace, you are so beautiful, you look so much like your mother." The old man could barely talk, but he grasped her hand and squeezed it gently. Grace looked down at him and smiled, tears streaming down her face. "I love you, Daddy."

Travis came over to his dad. His temples were graying but the rest of his hair was still jet black. He was a very handsome man, not very tall, but extremely handsome with that beautiful smile.

"Hi, Dad, are you feeling a little better?" Travis patted his father on his shoulder and squeezed his hand. He had developed a wonderful bedside manner, in part from his father, but mostly from the experience of his years as a top neurosurgeon in Atlanta. The old man gave his oldest son a proud smile and nodded yes at his oldest son's question.

"Glad you could make it, son." He whispered as he patted his son's hand. Then Trent came over to his father's side. Trent was now very tall and thin; a stock broker in New York. He must be about 40 by now. Grant looked into his sons eyes and gave a weak smile. "Dad, we've been pretty worried about you."

"Don't worry, son, I've had a good life." Grant said weakly.

Trent eyes began to water.

"Hey, Grant." The weak old man turned his head slowly on his pillow to his other side. Hunter and Jason were standing at his bed.

"We are happy to see you awake." Grant smiled at Jason. It almost seemed funny to hear him speak without his childhood speech impediment. They had grown up to be fine looking men. Both boys had their same sandy brown hair and their athletic bodies showed muscle through their knit shirts. Hunter had gone into the family business with his father and Jason had become a heart doctor and taken over the heart clinic in St. Charles for Grant when he retired.

Hunter stood silent, wishing he could say all of the things he wanted to say.

Jason was the one who spoke for both of them.

"Grant, we want you to know we couldn't love you anymore than if you were our own father."

Hunter then quietly said. Mother would have wanted us to thank you for giving so much of yourself to us, Grant."

Grant looked at all of his children. He managed to speak a weak "I love you all. I can't stay long, your mother is waiting for me." He squeezed Grace's hand and felt a comfort at having the children with him. He was grateful that he was able to tell them good buy.

His eyes fluttered and he drifted off to sleep again. The children all looked at each other, not understanding if the old man was incoherent or if there was a realistic meaning to what he just said.

"Grant; I'm here. Grant looked at Avery standing by the door. He felt wonderful. He threw the covers off of his body and went to meet her.

The children kept watch by his bed until they heard his last breath.

The early morning newspaper's obituary read as follows:

Dr. Grant Lee Jones of Saint Charles, Louisiana passed last night after a long illness. He was the founder of the St. Charles Heart Clinic. He is preceded in death by his wife, Avery. He leaves his five children: Dr. Travis Jones, of Atlanta, Ga., Trent Jones of New Orleans, La., Hunter Lyons of Baton Rouge, La., Dr. Justin Jones of St. Charles, La., and Hanna Grace Harper of Los Angeles, California, and eight grandchildren. He will be missed.

Printed in the United States
By Bookmasters